Divided Highway:

The Quest to Save the American Dream

Based on Actual Events

By: Daniel M Urbaetis

Contents, Table thereof:

Infamous Hiking Journal

Intro: **Typically found at the beginning**

The path to obscurity begins… They say there is the widely accepted truth, the higher truth, and beyond that—obscurity. Let's sit back, no! Let us sit at the edge of our respective seats, whether figuratively or literally, and gain a little something.

Through this learning there will be an unraveling. With this unraveling there will come a feeling of great discomfort invoked within the very core of our being. It is to be expected when wisdom brings us to a place beyond our zone of comfort, previous understanding, and acceptance.

Please remember, as it will bring surprising comfort to your otherwise tortured mind, that nothing is ever to be taken too seriously in the realm of Thought's existence. Understand the Grand Comedy for what it is and learn to be grateful for your position in its punch line. Remember too, those who dare this feat that separates Man, will <u>not</u> be alone in their journey.

Knowledge is the great, ancient barrier. It hinders our ability to see what truly Is, and what truly is of virtue, as spoken of in the tale of Adam and Eve. The common misunderstanding when reading the Old Testament is that the "God" figure did not want us to know what he did, and why he did it, thereby reducing His importance and power over us. Most people read this as "God" trying to preserve his own investment by disallowing Man to fully understand how he operates. This, my fellow travelers, is a misconception as ancient as the date in which it was written. "God" was trying to save us from ignorance.

He was trying to explain what a *fruitless* venture Knowledge truly was because all it can do is describe what and why things are what they are in the paper-thin comprehension of reality He created for us, and allows us to understand. What better symbol than an apple? He knew that "knowledge" of the School had little bearing on the Test that was being conducted. It was the original Distraction. He wanted us to be able to focus on our mission, our test, rather than be gifted in describing the water we were wading in, or the walls of our institutional hallways. Every other creature relies upon instinct and yet we're skeptics.

Knowledge teaches us not to trust it. We trot around calling ourselves the "intelligent life" all the time ignoring our intuitive nature. Apparently there isn't enough proof all around us, showing us otherwise. We're taught that long, arduous calculation is the path to the greatest results, but that is flawed thinking. Some elements do not require consideration for action to be taken.

This is a distraction from Higher Truth. Call it Science, or whatever. The fact remains, if you have little or immense knowledge in the things that matter the least, are you not still just wasting efforts describing those bulkheads that surround the boxes we are given?

It's the same as working for a company that recently hired someone to perform a job function. Imagine, if after a month of employment, all your employee can do is give a detailed, accurate description of the cubical assigned him. They can produce spreadsheet after spreadsheet weighing the pros and cons of having a window view, but can't do the work assigned. That is what "Knowledge" does for us. It discovers innovations within our box to make living within it more comfortable and *understandable*. That's like trying to make college dorm housing more inviting for a permanent stay. It is not a path to the Higher Understanding. If we had that person who could only describe their cubicles, rather than comprehend why they were there, shouldn't management want to fire them? If your answer is the same as mine then you, too will feel the fear I do being a Human. We're mixed up at the same *office* with the rest of this mob. I don't want to be "laid off" for being a bad, albeit Godly, experiment. It would all be due to the majority thinking they were brilliant, however, never truly comprehending anything.

God wants us to focus on the task at hand, not the simple math he created our world with. He's looking for people of worth to *have* with him. It must be lonely being Him. It's like having to deal with a Universe full of people whom you're smarter than and you know will never challenge you, intellectually. If God *is* looking for a friend, wouldn't you want to be it? Wouldn't you realize that describing things he already knows would be more of a bore to Him than an impressive way of showing your credentials?

Our vision is skewed by the belief that virtue comes from our advancements in <u>this</u> world. God wanted us to understand that this place is a given. The devil may just be another bully in science class with our "Lord" tormenting him until He can prove he's right, that His hypothesis is correct. This is a testing ground, just like the aforementioned college dorm. Hang a painting for the next guy, but don't waste all your efforts making it cozy. You still have a real task to focus on. Knowledge may not be the original sin, but it is the one that retards us in the eye of our creator. Let us look instead to Wisdom and intuition as Socrates did, although miniscule in comparison to where we all need to set the standard. The extending applications of Wisdom demand we pursue it.

When everything to be discovered by Wisdom is discovered there will be a clear door, a dimensional portal for us to walk through, labeled as "Layers" & "Size." It is one in the same door that opens our minds to the truest of all truths, making us feel small and prenatal. We will be as newborns, crying in terror of the world we're about to enter.

Both will challenge our accepted, common beliefs of our importance to "God" and of what is real. Neither can be discredited by the math we're so inclined to deem as the new divinity. We'll come to realize just how hollow our faith in that which can be eloquently explained by formula *is* when formulae have met the edge of existence.

As for the creators and carriers of formulae are concerned, they will be left with just as many questions as we, the "commoners" are. When seeking answers, one usually finds that the search, the path, leads to more questions. Why? "Layers." These layers need to be understood before they can be peeled back, revealing a deeper truth underneath. Wisdom, not knowledge, is the true path to understanding. Our reality is simply a layer among many.

Wisdom is the straight line to progress. Knowledge requires a very long, arduous path to which its findings finally discredit its own efforts and are thereby nullified. Which path do you wish to be on? One leads to a higher understanding and hopefully obscurity. The other that leads to a dead end is more difficult to reach, even though it's more socially acceptable. Emotion is the real science. Feeling and experiencing life is our only saving virtue, and the only worthy venture. I present to you, the Divided Highway…

A Message to You, Rudy

-The Specials

All right, before we get into it let's just diffuse the bomb that's bound to be mishandled by the media mongoloids. There are commonalities to a certain Hunter S. Thompson and myself, whom I dearly regard.

Thompson studied Radio Electronics in the Air Force. I studied Telecommunications in the US Coast Guard. It was a radio room position requiring Top Secret Clearance to acquire.

He landed on the *Command Courier* as their sports editor. I was the creative editor of my college newspaper, and I took it upon myself to draft a satirical publication for my fellow shipmates aboard the USCGC Alert.

We both petitioned for early release from military life, and found the confines of it to be unbearable. No man wants to be given orders by a halfwit. There are plenty of pride-driven halfwits in pressed uniforms calling the shots in every nook of all of the military branches.

Both of us are, were fascinated by travel and did as much as we could when the means were available.

We both have had to step outside of ourselves and say, "Calm down," with the same mistrust of our own words.

We are, were, both very self-assured. I seek no outside praise to assure myself of my gifts, abilities, and worth. I'm arrogant, but not pompous. I have the ammunition to back the wars I start, usually... I feel, as he did, constantly challenged by those seeking to kill all hopes of enlightenment. That is why I rise and fight. I am not about to give up on the potential of mankind or of myself.

His struggles early on, and his money troubles, reassured me that I was walking in the correct path. I too, have felt the woes of a creative mind. Family, friends, girlfriends, and even a fiancé have been harsh critics of my decisions and of my values.

The more I read about the man the more I'm almost taken aback by the similarities. This includes his philosophy of pushing your credit to its limits. Rest assured, I may have my heroes. My style, my form is all mine, however. I didn't know of Thompson until I was already experimenting with the pen, and doing it "My Way" as Frank Sinatra sang about. There's absolutely nothing wrong with admiring people in the same field of work as you. Everyone admires someone. It's as natural as shitting 30 minutes after eating Taco Bell.

As John Clease of Monty Python used to say, "And now onto something completely different..."

"I'm sick of doubt…"

-*James Douglas
Morrison*

"Just give him what he wants… Unless it's Eastern Europe."

-*Unknown*

"'Please be seated..?' I won't stand for this!"

-*Unknown*

"I was born a poor, black child…"

-Steve Martin, *The
Jerk*

September 9th, 2008

If you told me five short years ago that I would be where I am today, I would have recoiled in pure shock and anger. Even now, as I am waist deep in this situation, a large part of me is detached or otherwise in denial. How could this have happened? Why is the *driving force* propelling me in this direction? What is the purpose of this great test?

In 2004 I had just graduated from college. I finished strong with a 3.8 GPA that semester, and a 3.6 the semester before. With the maturity and life experience gained as a US Coast Guard I was able to focus, attack, and achieve in academics.

This was my time, my 15 minutes. I was going to set off to NYU and later become a paid, professional writer. I'm a planner and I had it all worked out upstairs just how things were to be done to maximize my potential for success. I was fresh from Acting I and II classes at the Maureen Stapleton Theater where I did everything from catwalk lighting and acting, to writing, and even directing a play. I was the Creative Editor of the *Hudsonian*, the college newspaper. I got my first taste of the journalistic lifestyle there and I ate it up like candy. The head editor recommended me for the position after having read my countless submissions. The board tasked me with finding the talent on campus and I accepted the challenge proudly. Later it was decided that my single page be expanded to three and I was to have full creative license. It marked the last time the staff and I were ever in agreement. I called my section, "Thoughtful Debris."

I had gone to a small, but respected community college in Upstate New York as a full-time student. I also worked full-time, forty or more hours weekly, at a convenient store. My duties were at the assistant manager capacity, therefore demanding more responsibility from me than the average crewmember. Between course work, job duties, and studying, little time was afforded for sleep. Yet, I made it. Not only did I graduate, I did so with recognition on the President's List for two consecutive semesters.

At a job fair I attended on a whim that August of 2004, I happened by a booth for a mortgage company. Later I would learn that it was the reincarnation of a business I worked for at age 19. I was their data entry specialist just before the Feds shut them down.

A very loud, outgoing gentleman, the kind you may find at a used car lot or hosting an obnoxious game show, was flailing his limbs in an attempt to wave me over to him. He spoke at a decibel level that was head rattling. I found the animation and energy emanating from his every movement intriguing, so I stepped in for closer examination. I was a kid who had no personal experience dealing with cocaine-driven individuals, yet. It was still a novelty to me.

In a plastic sincerity, he told me I looked like a sharp kid with a lot of potential. He asked me if my goals included making as much money as possible and quickly. When questions are asked in a certain way, there's only one honest answer that can be fired back. This is a sales strategy as old as the craft itself.

Here I am a fresh graduate with plans to go on to the next level of institutional learning facilities. I have ambitions of becoming the next Quentin Tarantino. Of course I wanted to make as much money as possible, but only if I could do it my way. I had an *all or nothing* mindset when it came to my writing aspirations. I was driven to write books, screenplays, theatrical plays, sitcoms, etc. I wanted to live my dream and the fresh accomplishments had given me enough confidence to believe I could do just that. After all, I've been a wise ass since I could speak. I've proven to be a well-spoken thorn in the side of every establishment I've ever engaged whether for my own personal amusement or otherwise. When I thought of myself in comparison to the bastards of standard practice, protocol, and tradition, I was way above their meaningless existences. I envisioned myself as the long bearded, white robed elder standing atop a jagged, rocky mountain shooting lightning bolts down at these people from my fingertips. No one could teach me anything I hadn't already deduced on my own or discovered through my extensive reading habit. I was self-driven, self-determined, and an easy target for a gifted salesman.

This portly guy with the groomed goatee and expensive suit was able to charm me from behind his podium. It was easy to see what a guy like me wanted. He massaged my ego, preyed upon my pride and had me locked in within a matter of seconds. He manipulated the proceeding conversation, albeit more of a lecture with a few rest stops for flattery. He intelligently sold me on the prospect of aiming my *divine lightning* at mortgage sales. I was aware of what was happening, but it was so interesting to witness him at work that I wasn't walking away. In fact, I was "slipping under the ether" as they say in the sales businesses. After all, he wasn't selling me a toaster with a built-in compass at some tradeshow. He was selling me Opportunity.

He saw me for what I was: a grand thinking, ambitious, arrogant little prick. He knew I wouldn't step down from my Pride long enough for even a moment of self-doubt. It didn't matter that I had no clue what a sales position at a mortgage company entailed, or even what it meant. Remember, I could do anything…

I signed the necessary paperwork right there at the kiosk, shook his metacarpal-crushing hand, and in an attempt to impress the man I tried saying, "thank you," at his octave level. It was half as deafening at best. There were a lot of people around, a lot of eyes. Maybe I was more timid than I would dare confess.

He said something like, "You're done. Get out of here. You have a job. Don't waste your time walking around to other booths. If you want to pick up girls go to the mall."

I shrank in stature as a wave of embarrassment broke over me. Now I couldn't stay. All the eyes, everyone must have heard his megaphone-voice. The announcement was clear, however inaccurate. I was marked as having an agenda outside of career hunting. Clever move, salesman. Manipulated yet again, I took to the doors in the most direct path I could navigate.

Before a total of 48 hours had elapsed, I was contacted for an interview by one of the mortgage company's appointment setters. I can't even tell you if I owned a single dress-shirt at the time. A late-night scramble to a department store solved that issue. I didn't go for the shirt-tie combo packs. Even then I saw them for what they are. It's a shortcut to having to think for yourself and match your clothes properly. It's a cheap fix and extremely awkward when passing someone who purchased the very same set.

There's less shame in a wrinkle-free number, so I snatched one up and matched it with a decent tie selection. This transaction forced me to spend the rest of what little cash I had.

Let me get back to my previous comment about being a "thorn-in-the-side" of the establishment. The underlying, driving decision that thrust me into a US Coast Guard uniform was not this *idea* of honor, nor was it to serve my country. It wasn't due to my father's encouragement to go off and do something noble. He proposed the idea everyday from the time I told him I met with a recruiter to the day I was at MEPS taking the ASVAB. It was because I felt I could gain something from the experience. I considered myself to be anti-government and anti-establishment in thought and ideals. I used to say, "I don't believe in nihilism, either." Something like this military business could be entertaining, if not educational.

The way I figured it, no one who feels so strongly in one particular direction would ever allow themselves to experience anything, but safe situations setup to reinforce the very ideals they hide behind. It's human nature to surround oneself with influences that favor their ideology. My contradicting belief was that I was an open-minded individual. All the time I was shutting out any challenging differences of opinion. I was a young man of firm conviction and my own set of values I'd argue for 'til death.

In an effort to derail myself from this path, I decided I'd enlist. I would join before I had a chance to stop myself. It was an impulsive choice. I acted in the exact opposite fashion of what a person of my belief structure should have. I broke the cycle and behold, a US Coast Guard was born.

To think the Federal Government unwittingly awarded me a Top Secret Clearance status almost sounds made up. These days, post 9/11, if I have too dark of a tan I'm asked to take off my shoes and bend over at the airport...

There I was, years later, rushing around and making sure everything was perfect for the "Man" in this game he calls the "Interview." I don't feel I need to tell the world that at age 24 I still couldn't do my own tie. I'll never confess that my mommy did it for me. I'll take that secret to the grave, thank you. On a completely unrelated topic, I love you, mom.

You may ask, "How did you do it in the Coast Guard?" They have a uniform that accessorizes with a tie called a Bravo. It's the formalwear at ceremonies and special events.

Well, when you're as resourceful as I am there's a way around everything. I had a fellow shipmate tie it for me. Every time the situation called for that particular selection of uniform I would simply pull the pre-tied knot over my head and tighten it. Later I'd loosen it back up enough to clear my ears and I'd take the damn thing off.

I still do that to this day. I've learned to tie my own double Windsor over the years, but I only tie them perfectly once. Following the same method as previously described, they never have to be tied again. Imagine how many hours, days, perhaps weeks I've added to my life that would otherwise have been consumed by this task. That's real innovation, my friends.

In my new silk tie with too small of a knot, a pair of Dockers that my mother probably purchased for me when I was in high school, and a pair of dressy, but unprofessional shoes by Steve Madden, I scooted over to the dreaded interview. Being anxious, I didn't sleep much the previous night and signs of fatigue were evident when I looked at my reflection in the rearview mirror.

I had what I considered to be a resume sitting beside me in the passenger seat. There's no measure for the level of professionalism you're at when you have your resume pressed in the first four pages of a spiral notebook. Who needs a briefcase? What use is a proper, clear plastic, resume cover? You're beyond all that. You're a superstar.

Every CEO looks back and remembers the beads of sweat that form on the brow when they arrive at their prospective employer's parking lot, turn off their car, reach for that all-too-clever solution to modern problems only to find a bent corner or a wrinkled edge. How could the spiral notebook system have failed them? It was so well thought out. They even printed out extra copies they didn't need just to reinforce the sturdiness. How much more innovative must a man be?

That split second where I contemplated driving back home and conceding the whole thing felt like a lifetime. Where did that cocky prick go that was roaming around the job fair? How would he handle this situation? I must have left him in a different spiral notebook somewhere.

I didn't wait long before I was called into an office. It was just enough time to absorb what I was up against as far as competition. Eight guys in mismatched clothes, I included, and one asshole who was all too perfect were crammed in a little room together. It was evident that the perfect guy wasn't just making me feel self-conscious. The other guys were looking themselves over. Some had puzzled looks on their faces as they scanned and re-scanned the information on their resumes. Me, I had a shortcoming from every category. I didn't know where to begin hating myself. Mr. Three-piece and his perfect, Italian leather briefcase were getting on my nerves. His very existence insulted me. I daydreamed that the other eight of us overtook him like a hungry school of piranhas and devoured him right down to his fancy fucking dress shoes. Alas, no such event occurred.

The interview itself was more like a session of Crossfire. Three suits sitting with me at a roundtable with another pacing behind them who said nothing the whole time, had me locked in a conference room. The space was large enough to breathe, but small enough to smell a bouquet of various fragrances. It was the culmination of all our colognes. Luckily, we all had taste. However, even fine scents can overpower the olfactory senses when combined with four others of equal strength and distinction. Before long I developed a burning, itchy sensation in my nasal passages.

I remember squinting a lot during the interview. The blinds were open on the window directly across from me, allowing maximum penetration of sunlight. The only time I had a moment of relief was when the pacing man would pass in front of the window. Occasionally he'd stand there briefly in just the right spot. Perhaps that was his intended function. He was operating the interrogation lamp, or in this case, the sun.

After about a 20 minute pep rally where they got all the *Hoorah!* answers they expected, they briefly touched on some vague aspects of what it means to be a mortgage consultant. They didn't go into detail as to what was required for success.

Just before they freed me, the mood, which previously was similar to being in the stands of a football game sandwiched between very enthusiastic fans, turned dramatically. The man to my right leaned in close and pointed at me with the cheap pen in his hand. "Do you think you can do this? Don't answer, yet. Do you think *you* can do this?"

I didn't even know what the hell; "this" was, let alone if I could actually do it. I sat there for nearly thirty minutes, and never once was there any mention of the job functions I'd be expected to carry out. Of course I gave them an enthusiastic, "Yes!" Maybe it was I who missed something. I could always ask what I'm supposed to do at a later time.

I had just made a statement, a proclamation that I would now have to deliver on. There were a total of five witnesses to this including myself. I was confused as all hell and I'm sure it was their intent.

"Your manager, Justin, will be along in a minute to introduce himself and ask whatever specific questions he has for you." Jesus Jones, it's not over, yet? "If he has no concerns or objections, could you make yourself available for next week's training class?"

That was the beginning of what would occupy my life for the next four and a half years. It was the birth of Daniel Michael Urbaetis, the mortgage consultant. I might not have bothered to balance my checkbook, or read the newspaper, but I was about to begin my practice of convincing people to make financial decisions based on my "expertise." Why not? With deregulation in full swing, I could tailor loans to fit mostly all of my borrowers' needs. After 90 days of employment, I was the last man standing from my training class of 19. They were either fired for lack of sales production or had quit before they could be.

It took me two months before I closed my first loan. That month I closed a total of four loans and took home just under six thousand dollars after taxes. The next month was even better. I went from a $10.48 per hour job at the convenience store to making a respectable, professional income. I bought a better car, one I had wanted rather than one I had to settle for. The previous year I was dependent on student loan excess to pay my rent and utilities.

My dream of becoming a writer didn't fade. That same year I finished my first screenplay. I called it, "LOGOS: A Mock Epic." To this day no one in the business of producing films has ever seen it. Many of my friends have read it and urged me to try and sell it. That's a lot easier said than done, I've learned.

After a long time trying to understand why a man with an original piece of semi-fictional, comedic brilliance had no agency representation, I shifted my focus to the profession that was filling my refrigerator with fine-cut steaks and seafood. So began the tug-of-war I struggle with everyday.

Occasionally I say, "Fuck this! I'm a writer!" It's usually followed by a burst of creative activity, but just as often it's followed by a burst of vomit and an unpleasant cab ride home. If someone asked me why I drink, I'd be honest. I know of few ways to achieve belligerence without it. When these periods of high activity hit me every word flows out as if it has just been released from prison. I feel most alive in these times. It is as if I have given meaning and purpose to my existence. I sense that I'm writing my way through a path to an even greater solution, a self-discovery of sorts. Maybe it's just around the next punctuation or beyond the next syllable. It's within sight, but just far enough out of reach to further fuel my efforts as I tirelessly pursue it with eager mind and grasping hands. Energy radiates from the pen until it glows with a white-hot intensity. Smoke emits from every keystroke. I'm right where I always want to be: somewhere between the problem and the solution, or solutions. It's all up to me. The story goes where I choose and there are countless choices to be made in every body of work.

It's been over four years since I wrote the screenplay. I can read it cover to cover with the same excitement I had when it was first printed and bound. I didn't even know the proper format for it, so I wrote it free-flowing, and with complete control. There I go again, sticking a thorn in the side of *tradition*. When I revisited it, I discovered the only element that it lacked was a contents page.

There are times when I come up with advertising slogans for existing products, or produce my own quotes. The quotes are what I call, "fortune cookie wisdom." They don't build a story, but could be used in future dialogue. If I had a screen-printing business I could apply that wit and make lots of humorous t-shirts like the kind seen everywhere these days.

As for the tug-of-war, there are many times I felt and feel like I have to make a choice between the life that demands my attention and the life I want to devote my efforts to. I'm always at odds with this. There's responsibility, tradition, career pressures, and even the nesting instinct set in opposition to things like passion, dreams, and the urge to take the road less traveled by. Those with clearly defined aspirations, dreams and goals have a much harder time dealing with compromise and substitution. Who wants rolled Pollock when they have tasted real crab?

Anyone who's walked a mile in the mortgage salesman's shoes knows its cycle all too well. There are more ups and downs than a roller coaster ride. It's not for the faint of heart or the weak of stomach. When you're up, you're way up, so high you can't even smell your own shit. When you're down, you're way down, seen as inferior by your colleagues, and you can't seem to produce a single nickel of profit. Companies don't let you stay down too long before they fire you. The common expression is, *"What have you done for me, lately?"* Managers have this mentality in just about every professional field involving sales.

Picture this scenario. I could have had three exemplary months in a row, had been the immediate supervisor's golden child, and maybe that made me a little too confident or comfortable. This month my numbers are way down and I have yet to convert anything solidly. I had the *feast* now prepare for the *famine* because it's coming, and fast.

To have been with the same company for well over three years is an impressive statement for this line of work. Not only is it testament to my production, but also to my stress management abilities during these peak-and-valley times. I left on my own terms after having helped the company establish their first satellite office. I was the top producer for the first month in the new team's headquarters. After it was apparent that a management opportunity was going to a lesser producing friend of the AVP, I started planning my exit strategy.

Besides, I could see the smoke before the fire. The AVP tasked with running the shop was way out of his league. He began his career during the *refi-boom's* most active period. Back then there were little sales skills needed and even less knowledge of the business required to be successful. Phones rang with incoming calls more than they were used to make outgoing contacts. People were filling orders, not selling. There were countless products available for people with all types of income and credit categories. Paper was traded with ease and considered to be worth something, so everyone wanted to lend.

Lenders couldn't draft documents and disclosures fast enough to keep up with the aggressive demand. Appraisers and title companies were flooded with business requests. People were converting their mortgages, sometimes carrying a double-digit interest rate from a previous era, into rates as low as 5% or better. Tell me, what sales skill does one really need to possess to make saving thousands of dollars sound like a good idea?

That was where my AVP was birthed. By the time he was working in the Florida office with me he was far out of touch with reality, but he had plenty of rhetoric and grandiose plans that looked pretty on paper. I knew he was doomed after witnessing him in action, *second-voicing* a few of my loans. I had better find a way to avoid repeating that experience if I was ever to make another dollar at that company. Some of those clients, whom I had a great rapport with up to that point, never answered their phones for me again.

We parted ways in May of 2007. I had been calling-off frequently and lying out by the pool in my apartment complex. The way I saw it, I'd get just as many loans closed if I was drunk by noon as I would if he insisted on scaring away all of my borrowers. A few months later I learned the shop was closed. Headquarters knew they had made a mistake and were sick of wasting resources on a fruitless endeavor. Just like that, five people including my former AVP were unemployed. I mean just like that! It was so instant and without warning that it was almost cruel.

The IT department was given the order to cut the feed and that was that. Five people saw their computer screens go down as their virtual connection to HQ was severed. The phones were dead, everything. It was all part of the same network being supported by the New York office. The AVP had to call from his own mobile phone to find out what had happened. It wasn't an accident or an IT issue. They were being let go. With that phone call in the annals of history, my former AVP went from making a little over eleven thousand dollars monthly to making nothing at all. His newly finished, but certainly by no means paid for, 5,000+ square foot home was now in jeopardy. I had visited that home. In all his false modesty, I was given the grand tour. I didn't feel as bad for him as I did his children. The wife can work, he can go back to whatever construction nonsense he was doing before hand, but the kids had a dream house that all kids would want to grow up in. They would be forced to say goodbye to it and all of its promise for the future.

He lived and died by the sword. That is the nature of the sales world. It's social Darwinism in its purest form. It could be argued that he was never able to keep ahead of the change and maybe he was rolled beneath its tires. Things didn't work his way, anymore. To me it's completely irrelevant. He never had any business being a salesman, but he didn't know that. That was the real problem. Early success made him think he had found his niche. When it came time to exercise real sales skills, however, his palms were open, facing the heavens and he had a look of confusion painted all over his face.

It wasn't just about putting the borrower under the ether, anymore. Lenders were just as much an opposing force as an excitable prospect. Market retraction caused products to leave the shelves, and programs to disappear sometimes while in mid-processing. Imagine owning a bakery and all you have left to sell is white bread. Half your clients eat only honey wheat, and another group needs rye. "Sorry, if you don't eat white bread I can't help you. My hands are tied." Try making a living in that environment.

Self-employed, Stated programs became taboo where they were once a huge slice of the pie, and so on… The examples are endless and the restrictions are continuing to tighten. Companies who survive this historical event will have little competition awaiting them on the other end. The question is, how do human beings with families, or otherwise, live through this downturn long enough to see the light promised at the tunnel's end? An intestine is tunnel like in nature, too. Right now we're all wading in the shit-filled tube.

To put it in perspective, January 2008 I took home $9,280 in total. I was the top producer for the month at a particular company. I sold only one loan the following month. I took initiative and sought employment elsewhere. It wasn't because I was making excuses for myself, or blaming the economy. I really just wanted to take the money I made, the money they forced me to wait until March, almost 60 days to finally receive, and focus on my writing for awhile.

The most recent mortgage company I worked for I made almost nothing. I was unable to get a loan approved from mid May 2008 to August of 2008. I had plenty of loans in my pipeline, but the problem was getting the lender to clear the files for closing. There was also a horrible marketing system in place fueled by salesgenie.com. You may as well open a phone book and start dialing. There was more legwork involved because there was no such thing as a prescreened lead there—no filters. My life, my career, and the family I was trying to provide for were all sinking into the abyss. I made $1,000 per month as a base salary. I felt bad taking that much because I never made it back for them.

What's more cheerful was, during the same time, my fiancé and I were fighting eviction. We had been renting a nice little 1,604 square foot home in suburbia, Tamarac, FL. The homeowner renting us the property had not paid his mortgage for months before we signed our lease and moved in. We entered the home a little before Christmas time. By the end of March we had a surprise visitor. A loss mitigation representative, hired by Countrywide, stopped by for a chat. It was a very informative visit. She gave us more details than she was legally at liberty to, but seeing that were a young family, her heart went out to us. Thus she will remain nameless.

Up until that visit, we had no reason to suspect that the house we lived in was in jeopardy of any sort. Being in the business in no way made me immune to the very woes of clients who came to me too late. The generation of mortgage lenders and brokers that my former AVP represented were responsible for this epidemic. That's not to say that borrowers were not equally as guilty with their impulsive, ignorant approach to their own finances. They signed the paperwork. The conditions were all there in writing. Just because you can get something doesn't mean you should have it. I guess three years, two years, whatever seemed too far ahead into the future to worry about an increase in payment. I can hear the rationalization, "Well heck, if it was this easy to get a loan I'll just refinance again when the rate expires."

I don't quite remember the date in late May when it happened, probably because I don't want to. After a two-month battle involving the court system of Broward County, my landlord, and the looming prospect of foreclosure, we were served an eviction notice. We had fought to get our money back for all of the rent paid due to the landlord's inability to provide a stable living environment for the term agreed on in the lease. We put our rent money in the hands of the court until a decision could be reached. The courthouse had a mountain of cases like ours to process. Instead of paying attention to the details, they arrived at the most simple of solutions. They evicted us and awarded our landlord the rent money. Just like that we were out of funds we could have used to pay security and rent on a new place. We had four miserable days to make other arrangements, pack up everything we owned, and clear out of the property. We still had to go to work, and do the normal things that demand people's time.

There's no feeling quite comparable to one that swelled up and choked out my heart when I looked over the faces of Alice's four children, and had to explain what was happening. I treated them like they were my own. We lived together like a family. I think I ended the teary scene with something like, "I'm sorry guys. We need you to spend time with your grandfather while mommy and I pack." Their sanctity had been taken away and I was powerless to prevent it. Nothing prepares you for that emotion. I couldn't look my own fiancé in the eye. We didn't just lose a home. We lost what that home symbolized for our future together.

I was in shock and disbelief, but it became pretty damned real after I placed the last box of belongings into the moving pods.

Alice, her four beautiful children, and I took refuge at her father's house a few blocks away. My time there was numbered before I even set foot across the doorway. Why wouldn't it be? What right did I have to be there in the first place?

There were other reasons for this. Harry was a very angry man with a clinical mental condition. Whether he takes his medication or not, Harry has the potential of behaving like a Monster both verbally and physically. The man punched me in the face once because I decided to call on some files at work and got home a little late. I was taking off my tie when he came storming in, and hit me. As he was kneeling on my chest and choking me he kept repeating, "You're no good. You're no good," not like the song, but more like the uttering of a man in a blind rage.

By August things between Harry Monster and me had reached a boiling point. From his perspective, he saw nothing wrong with the outbursts. So long as he mustered up a half-hearted apology, all would be forgiven. I wasn't buying it and I was tired of the cycle. I have a permanent scar on my jaw line from the last time he hit me. My stubble grows into the scar instead of out. Every so often Alice would tweeze out several long black hairs that were growing under my skin.

Needless to say, I desired a change, but I felt trapped because I wasn't making any money. Subsequently, I had just been laid off from the mortgage company that previous Friday. By Sunday I tasted change. There was an ugly scene, and I felt it best for Alice and the kids if I stayed away.

There was never any telling what Harry Monster was capable of when he failed to take his medication. The argument that resulted in a few blows being exchanged occurred over Harry's attempt to kill our family dog, Abigail. I watched as this 244 pound man swung my 32 pound dog like a baseball bat into the tree she was tied to, head first. As if that wasn't enough he then picked my dog up with both hands, raised her over his head, and power-slammed her into the ground. As he did this he dropped to his knees so as to apply as much force as possible. All of his weight was put into the action. I sprung off a couch in the garage, where I was sitting with Alice, and charged him like a speeding locomotive. Fire was burning in my eyes as I shoulder blocked him as hard a man 100 pounds his lesser could. It knocked him for a backwards somersault resulting in his grass stained shirt and bloody nose.

As he got to his feet, with a stunned expression on his face that didn't last very long, he began ranting. "I don't like when dogs play like that! Do you want her jumping all over people?"

The dog had been excited to see him, and like most excited dogs, Abigail started doing the happy dance around him. That's what he referred to as "jumping all over." What Abigail did wasn't nearly as dramatic as Dino's response when Fred would come home. Imagine if there was a Flintstones episode where Fred ended up killing Dino with his bare hands in front of the rest of the family. That is what this lunatic was trying to rationalize.

After a few moments of pacing, in an offensive posture, waiting to see what he was going to do next, I relaxed a little and decided that it might be a good time for me to leave. As I was walking away I felt an impact at the base of my skull. The son-of-a-bitch threw a cheap punch when I was clearly in no way a threat. My back was to him for Christ's sake. Bruce Lee would have been so disappointed. "Never take your eyes off your opponent, even when you bow."

I turned around and swung a left hook that connected directly with his ear on his huge, fat head. I don't think his skull moved a millimeter in any direction, but according to Alice's report many days later via phone conversation, Harry Monster received a total of 17 stitches in both inner and outer portions of his ear. The medical doctor informed Harry that it would remain cauliflower permanently. The only thing I thought I did was bruise my hand on his rock-head. With that little Jerry Springer moment behind me, a member of my family was safe from harm, furry as she may be. I however, was officially homeless. Police were dispatched soon after I left the property and rounded the first corner. I could hear the sirens, police officers talking to one another, and then nothing. They had gone back to the scene or just gave up the search and drove off. Meanwhile, a few well-executed maneuvers aside, I was hiding behind a dumpster strong in my convictions and certainly in no mood to go to jail that day.

When I was as sure as I could ever be that the interest in my capture had faded, I began walking, north, then south down a different road and back north again. It was my belief that the erratic path would make my chances of getting out of the county unseen much greater. You don't commit a bad act and then walk straight down the main artery of town. You can, but you'd be a fucking idiot. Eventually I met up with State Road 7, or 441, and walked clear out of Broward County and into Palm Beach County. 19 hours of walking later, I stepped into a mall in Wellington, FL. I had to buy new shoes. The pair I was wearing was worn out well before I took this little trip. My feet, covered in blisters, screamed out for mercy and the muscles in my legs were ablaze.

After acquiring a very comfortable, twenty dollar solution to my problem, I sat down awhile on one of the cozy mall chairs. It was an incredible, relaxing experience. Realizing how much pain I was in when I tried standing back up, I felt it would be best if I made it over to the VA Medical Center of West Palm Beach. I had to walk another four hours or so to get within range of the hospital. The trip was much less painful on my feet with the new shoes, but my legs were constantly cramping. By the time I made it there, I was barely walking at all. I was taking short, old-man steps. My back was now starting to cause problems for me, too. Between the after-hours ER entrance and myself, stood a formidable hill, considering I was in Florida. Well, fuck it. I guess if I want resolution I'll have to work for it. This would be my final test. I felt like the *Gunslinger* in Stephen King's book series, "The Dark Tower." At least, I would have if I had any spare energy to entertain such fantasies. From an outsider's perspective it must have looked like a one-man geriatric race. I was humming along at the speed of injured turtle. At one point I kept repeating, "Ow," with every step. It was said in defiance. I remember thinking, "It's real funny that I happen to find the one hill in all of fucking Florida in one of it's flattest counties. Good one, Lord. You better not kill me, because if you do, I'm going to come up there and poke you right in your fucking eye! Then we'll see who's laughing."

Even at that moment I didn't think I was in dire need of any real medical attention. My purpose for having gone there in the fist place was just to see whether I was still eligible for medical benefits from my service as a Coast Guard, in the event I needed something in the future. I'm sure it didn't take me more than several minutes to reach the crest of the summit, but to me it may as well have been days.

After verifying I still had benefits, I switched my primary care information to their facility with a few minutes of Q & A. The duty nurse was a little concerned for my well being and ordered a series of blood tests just to be on the safe side. I spent the next eleven days at their facility with a condition known as rhabdo, or something that sounded a lot like that. I was in a state of delirium and couldn't quite comprehend the words being uttered to me. All I picked up from the nurses that passed by was that I was experiencing a high level of muscle tissue breakdown and if the levels continued to increase in my bloodstream it would threaten my kidneys and other vital organs. Basically, I could slip into a state of complete system shutdown. Apparently my spleen was enlarged as well.

A day or two later, when I had had some rest and was more capable of focusing on conversations, I explained my situation. I informed them of Alice, the last few months of events and how I was recently made jobless and homeless. Later, I would find out through a phone call that Harry Monster was threatening to kick Alice out on the street if she had any further contact with me. He said he'd put his own grandchildren in foster care and quote, "just be done with the whole thing." A single, homeless mother would have no recourse in that situation and the things she loves the most, the things that make her who she is, would be stolen out from underneath her never to be seen again.

The staff took pity on me, but it wasn't something I asked for. I felt like an imposter, unworthy of the hospital bed I was taking from some ominous, more deserving inhabitant. There were people coming home from Iraq with missing parts and here I am, just some retarded homeless guy. I'm watching the VA's television and eating food that could have gone to a brave veteran. I was beside myself with frustration and personal disgust.

I know from roaming the hospital with my I.V. on wheels, that in the basement level reside many Vietnam Era veterans in the nursing home. In their golden years, when they should be out yachting the globe, they're learning a cold, hard fact of life.

Diabetes is a far deadlier, less forgiving adversary than any bomb or mortar they ever encountered. It steals away their limbs a piece at a time, causes blindness, and in extreme cases, even leads to DEATH.

For those of you following along at home here's a brief summary of how my life had changed in less than two year's time. I went from buying my dream camcorder, a Panasonic AG-DVX-100B, a camera that had the capability of shooting at 24 frames per second; the same speed theatrical films are shot in, to having to pawn it for $1,200. I paid a little over $2,800 for it. Included in that price were an extended life battery, an Azden shotgun microphone, and some other various accessories. With it went my dream of putting together a few scenes from my screenplay for marketing purposes. In January of 2005 I walked onto a car lot, pointed at the car I wanted, and in a day I was driving it home. Compare that to waking up one morning for work and peering outside my Florida home's window only to find a bunch of muddy ruts in my yard made by the Repo Man. He dragged my beloved vehicle away in the middle of the night. I never saw the car again. I had an extensive collection of DVDs, some of which were out of print. They were all pawned for a dollar apiece. I got a whopping fifty cents per compact disc I pawned. In the end I had basically given away over 250 CDs and 135 movies for pennies on the dollar. With each transaction I wasn't just losing things. I was losing a piece of my soul, for those items helped form my beliefs and enhanced my life tremendously. They were my friends. They inspired confidence in me that I would one day make it in my chosen realm of artistic expression. What I pawned was my hope. I did it cheap, but it was a priceless, painful ordeal every time.

The doctors and social workers teamed up and found me a place to reside, temporarily. It was a halfway house. Normally it's reserved for *recovering* drug addicts, ex-cons finding roadblocks in their efforts to seek employment, and the mentally ill. A lot of the inhabitants fit into more than one of these categories. People go there to hide from the world after realizing that their best efforts can't hide them from themselves. Being there was a disgrace, but I was grateful nonetheless.

I'm packed into a four-man room with three degenerate crack heads, roach and rat infestations, and plenty of gang members and drug using prostitutes just outside the gated entrance. I receive less government aide, none in fact, because I don't have a substance abuse problem. How's that for bitter irony? There are no government programs for guys with bad luck. Because I didn't intentionally setout to fuck my life up, I'm on my own. A guy who smokes crack and steals from his mother has all the help in the world. I've been at the Carrington Center now since August 15th. Today is technically the 10th of September, the eve of a very dark day in history. I still can't find a job despite my best efforts to do so. All I've been able to accomplish is enrolling in a chef apprentice school at a local outreach center. My impressive resume has only led to oblivion. Not even a simple fast food position has been offered, and I've scoured the entire town ready to take any job I could get. The VA paid for the first $175 of my rent here. I'm supposed to come up with $150 dollars every week to remain here. $600 is more than I paid for the apartment I lived in for over three years in New York. That's a lot of money to live in a place where I'm constantly worried about what little belongings I have being stolen. Most would understand my aforementioned state of denial. A lesser man would probably have gone insane. Who knows? The day has just begun.

The American Dream Walk

"I've seen a few men down
the road of the righteous
and just a few have traveled
it's a lonely path..."

-Dropkick Murphys

"And whosoever compels you to go a mile, go with him two..."
-Matthew 5:41

I've tasted success. It's been in my possession. Even if it hadn't, I have too many plans, too many goals to just sit back and let things happen. I make my own path. I'm a warrior! "I'm Gumby, dammit!"

Being in the mortgage business I've probably heard the term used a million times. "The American Dream, the American Dream..." It resonates in my head. It used to stand for the belief that a person could accomplish anything in this country so long as they worked hard enough. The only limit placed on what one could achieve was decided by their own imagination and their will. That is what it meant in the Gold Rush Era. Pioneers of a new frontier risked their lives, migrated thousands of miles, for a chance to strike it rich. It's never about the money, but the freedoms that money unlocks that drive us. Considering the dangerous journey these brave men and women trekked, it would be silly to think of it in terms of a get-rich-quick scheme. Families were literally dying for the idea of a better life just beyond the next mountain. It's much more noble than today's substitute located on a desert strip in Nevada.

The term, *American Dream*, evolved. It's the same concept discussed in the United States Constitution. Commonly associated with the fundamental principle that every man and woman has the right to own property, raise a family, and further strengthen the nation at large, the *Dream* became the house. Whether you crave a white picket fence, a healthy green lawn, a friendly mailman who always has a free moment to chat, or a beach condo in Miami, the idea is the same.

I was funding the *American Dream* for a few great years. There were many families whom I helped, or at least played a crucial part in realizing their goals. Even if it wasn't a purchase, I still assisted in reducing their monthly expenditures thereby increasing excess funds. I walked them down a path that led to a better quality of life they didn't require a raise to achieve.

It was mid June of 2008 when finances began to get real tight and the trips to the pawnshop became a part of my life. I was seeing the hardship everywhere, not just in my microcosm. It was all the news anchors could talk about. Words like "downturn" and terms like "housing crisis" were repeated on a skipping record. It was very clear that jobs, banks, and homes were all under fire. Slap ridiculous petroleum prices on top of that and we had ourselves an epidemic. Other people were losing more than I ever gained in the first place. Which is a good point in and of itself: The more you have, the more you have to lose. "What can be done," I wondered. I didn't feel alone, but that came as no great comfort. We were all looking to the heavens, looking to our banking institutions, and in an act that can only be viewed as the final straw of desperation, looking to our government for some kind of answer, some measure of hope. To some of the more religious, I'm sure it felt like even He was shrugging his robed shoulders as confused as the lot of us. What future, if any, could be salvaged from this? Who had the answers?

These questions plagued me more and more as loan after loan was held up in underwriting, or otherwise denied all together. I was going mad. I had a fiancé with children to think about, and I had no money to get us out from underneath the thumb of her father.

Alice and I fought a lot more often. When it comes to dealing with women, I've learned they have a unique gift for the art of argument. They know just what to say to make a man feel degraded, and inferior. It wasn't like she had to look far with my career in the downward flush. And she was great at stripping away my dignity like a bandage on a child's knee. At first there's the shock, then your brain catches up with its pain receptors. I'll never understand how a person who's supposed to be in love could intentionally make me feel that horrible. If she really believed the terrible opinions she expressed, why the hell did she ever utter words like "love" and "forever?" Ah, women... They're life's great Distraction. Everything's the man's fault and if it isn't he'll be blamed anyway. Sit back, smile, and eat shit because there's not a damned thing we can do about it. They are like Social Security. You'll pay into them all your life and when it comes time for your return, there'll be nothing there.

It was on or around July 3rd when Alice and I had a huge argument and this time Harry Monster entered the ring in her corner. Normally, I'll battle wits with anyone and everyone. I have strength in my convictions and no one is worthy of the honor of trying to rewire my head with a different set of values or beliefs. This time however, I let them do the shouting. I simply walked outside and headed down the road. If arguing gets us nowhere and violence usually ends the night, why not really piss them off and not play into their trap? I wasn't sure how many more punches my jaw could take.

As I was walking I felt the knots of stress loosen. My mind was free to wander and think about something other than the horror show at the homestead. Now, instead of a massive coronary, I might feel my heart pump for a healthy reason. I gazed up at the stars as I made my way through the community. Everything seemed so grand and peaceful. It was a peace I hadn't felt in... I couldn't remember.

That's when it hit me. With little regard for fixing my own, immediate problems, I thought a little bigger. It was almost too simple in theory and it just might be what this country is screaming for. An act, a symbol... Our country needed a complete overhaul of the nonsense the media was constantly shoving in our faces. The idea that the *American Dream* was dead, was the most sinister seed ever planted in our minds. Hope, dreams, and concepts are never dead because they do not originate outside of us. They are created from within. They are our souls, and they are what fuel our engines with desire for more than that which is too easily obtained. Who the fuck is the media to proclaim that the soul of

Man is dead? Why, because they say so or because they want us to feel that way, to feel helpless?

What were we missing? It wasn't as complex as I first tried making it. All we were asking for was someone to step forward and lead the way. Don't be frightened. I read history. I'm not trying to say we needed a Mussolini, or a Hitler to lie to us more and lead us down a path to Hell, ever preying on the initial desperation that made such a movement possible in the first place. We just needed something to believe in. What better *something* than us as Free, Independent Americans?

"Why not be the voice I've been looking for," I pondered. If I could inspire my fellow countrymen to once again be proud to be Americans, wouldn't that lead to positive change? When this country was first founded WE Americans were proud to designate ourselves as such. There was a certain air of smugness about us and it was rightly justified. We need to regain that pride. Rather than sitting back, frightened, and awaiting the miracle that will never come, why not take charge of our lives and make the change happen? It takes courage, pride, honor, and all the other inherent qualities we as Americans have to accomplish said mission. We've got the tools, baby. Let's see what we can build with them.

First we need an act that will draw attention to itself. We need to couple that with active involvement by anyone who would like to feel like they're a part of it. We the People, need to all share something so that everyone's voice can be heard and recorded. We need a figure, a person, to carry the torch through this outlandish act for us to relate with. We need to realize that this act is a symbol of inspiration far more important than the man who led the initial part of the movement. We need to get off our asses and make something good with the rest of the time we've got because GODAMMIT, WE'RE AMERICANS, and we don't go down that easy. In a *Bronx Tale* there's mention about how there's nothing worse than wasted talent.

Thus the concept for the **American Dream Walk** was born. If a two-mile walk could inspire me this much imagine what a walk from Ft. Lauderdale, FL to Venice Beach Boardwalk, CA could do for me, and the country! I would walk all the way across country if it meant I could empower even one fellow countryman to tap into the ancient vein that once made our country strong.

When I got back *home* things were quieter than anticipated. I should have been leery of it, but my mind was elsewhere. I hurried myself passed the fiancé without saying a word and opened up our laptop. I found the distance from starting point "A" to ending point "Z" to be roughly 2,740 miles. From research I learned that the average human walks about 2.5 to 3 miles per hour, giving variance for length-of-stride, and cargo load. 2,740 miles should take a total of 1,096 hours to complete at the stated average pace. If I regimented a solid eight hours of progressive walking each day, I'd be done in 137 days. I factored in such things as fatigue and troublesome weather delays. Barring any other unknowns, I set my goal at 150 days. I learned quickly that certain roads, such as interstate arteries, are technically illegal to walk along. My trip wasn't something that could be planned using Map Quest. I had to plot a course using the most walker-friendly routes. With eight states to consider, this was no small task. Especially when all I had to do was look at a road map to see how picture-perfect and direct Interstate 10 would be if I were able to consider it an option. It cut through the southern states, nicely. The law was mocking me.

With a basic concept of the actual trip in mind I turned my attention to other the other elements that had to be represented. If I wanted to get people involved, what could be better than to find a way to invite them along? If only for a few miles, it's the symbol, and the understanding of it that matters most. Maybe I could get on TV or place ads in the newspapers. I could use media against itself to send out something with a positive message for a change. Now to assure that everyone who wants their voice heard *is*, I could invite them to send me an e-mail with a dream or goal they are living, are striving for, or felt they've lost touch with. I could later print out what I've collected and have it bound at an office store. I'd call it the "Dreams Binder" and I'd carry it with me the whole way. Literally, I'd be carrying the dreams of Americans on my back. Fuckin' A! As for drawing the attention away from me, the individual, I could use an item as a symbol of something far more important. I would need a bag to carry my survival supplies in, anyway... Why not use my military issue C bag I got when I was in the US Coast Guard? It has been years since my tenure, but I held onto it. Shit, I've thought about packing that thing up on more than one occasion just to get away from the circus that is Harry Monster's house. This way, people will see the bag as a representation of my service, the strength of our military, of sacrifice, and of or country as a whole. …Or they might just see it as a big green monkey on my back, but I could roll the dice on this one.

September 19th, 2008

    I haven't had a dollar in my pocket since August 15th. For whatever reason, my hometown used to conduct a fireworks display every year on that date. I'm no longer there as witness to stake any claim regarding its continuance.

    If it weren't for this halfway house I'd be completely homeless, and probably killed within minutes on the surrounding streets. Riviera Beach is just up the road. If you're goal is to find a prostitute, a drug, or a quick bullet, that's your place. People always talked about West Palm Beach as if it was the ideal vacation spot for rich tourists. North Palm Beach, maybe... Singer Island, all right it has its redeeming qualities. Every nook in between including West Palm itself is a cesspool. I wouldn't bring a family within five miles of Broadway any time of the day. I live right off of it. Without a penny for the bus, it's a profound mystery as to why this white-boy, walking all by his crazy lonesome, hasn't disappeared yet. I've had some very scary run-ins, but so far I've been able to survive. I guess there's some truth to that whole *Daniel in the lion's den* concept.

    I remember one day in particular. I was walking towards the KFC up the road to beg for a job. They had my resume and told me they were looking for one nightshift person. I hounded them everyday for two weeks. This day was no different. A little less than midway along my half-mile journey I came across three police cars that were wedged in an automotive center's entrance. As I passed by I happed to glance over. Who can resist that brand of morbid curiosity? Sitting there on the asphalt with his back against one of the police vehicle's passenger doors, was a Guatemalan covered in knife wounds and bleeding into his own lap. The cops surrounding him were completely emotionless. It wasn't disturbing, nor exciting to them. In fact, they appeared bored with the scene as they stood by and let the man suffer. I'm only 5'5", maybe 5'6" on a good day. This little foreigner was portly and much shorter. Whoever sliced him all up must have either been a rabid midget whom felt threatened, or a very cowardly gentleman, indeed. This, mind you, was in the middle of the afternoon on a bright South Florida day.

Conditions within these walls are no better than out there. At least you can hide in a dumpster or walk a different way if you spot trouble on the streets. In here I'm forced to interact and make small talk with some very dangerous, and otherwise retched human beings. They're called roommates. In a perfect world, I would stay as far from these people and their business as possible. Regrettably, I do not have that option. Theft is as common as breathing is in my shared room. If they aren't taking, I have the low life motherfuckers waking me up, sometimes before dawn, begging me for change I don't even have for myself!

As it stands I only eat a few days a week and when I do I'm eating free bread donated from a local baked goods store. It's not exactly a bakery, but more of an outlet. They deliver outdated and soon-to-be outdated food to us, here. I'm literally living on bread and water. Sundays are drop-off days. By Wednesday my one-loaf ration is usually long gone, especially considering the theft problem I mentioned. I drink a lot of water on days I have no food just so I can feel some sensation of fullness. I have to say, poverty is great for the abs. The couple stubborn pounds I was never able to get rid of when I wasn't destitute have shed off quick as lightning. Last I checked I weighed 122 pounds fully clothed. A chain of grocery stores known as Publix, or *Pubix* to me, all have a scale just beyond the first set of automatic doors leading into their establishments. They're great big things that look like they may have been the height of technology during the days of the World's Fair in New York. Of course, no store would place valuable antiquities where every moron could walk on them. They're replicas, probably used by some gung-ho security guards they have lurking around the store. They probably weigh suspected shoplifters on these scales to see if they've gained any weight since arrival. Shit, I have a conspiracy theory for just about everything...

It's 4:21 in the morning and there's no more sleep to be had. My bunk bed isn't the most comfortable of arrangements and the other assholes snore. I find myself here, in the common space of the house, often. As I peer out this grimy, old window into the parking lot it's difficult to comprehend the accomplishments I've made toward my endeavor. I labored day after day on the American Dream Walk details from planning and preparation, to endless searching for sponsorship with the aide of many a library's computer and a simple phone. Alice, that beautiful, intelligent woman of mine suggested I develop a website to host the event. That way I could direct any prospective business to it and they'd have all the relevant details. The website was originated on July 22nd as www.adw2740.com. I poured my best efforts into making it very well written and presentable. It's hosted by a bunch of Yahoos, good people. This came eight days after my first media coverage.

It was a two-minute and fourteen-second spot on two separate news stations that night. CBS 4 and MY 33 are related, so both were able to give me airtime. All this came about in a very unexpected fashion. I had used the mortgage company's computer and printer to draft flyers about the event with its originally scheduled date of August 28th, my birthday. I asked local businesses if I could tape the flyers up and thereby spread the word. One place, a gym that was near my office, had a member of the media as a client. He read my flyer that management was kind enough to allow me to post and later Mr. Codd contacted me via e-mail. The message included a phone number for me to reach him at, directly. I again used company resources and called him from my office. After about six minutes of very pleasant banter, we agreed on a five o'clock appointment that very day outside of my place of employment. It took forty-five minutes of interview to extract the short, however flattering, piece. I came home with a glow as if I had just had a religious experience. It was finally real to me. This just might work and there was no question in my mind whether I was crazy or stubborn enough to pull it off. Alice's kids got a kick out of seeing me on television. It was a very heartwarming moment for a guy who'd felt inferior and ashamed in their eyes for far too long. This segment produced a whopping eleven e-mails wishing me luck and informing me of my inspirational impact on their day. It was a start, anyway.

What were Alice and the kids to do in my absence? Who would provide the other 50% of the bills and the love needed to keep a family going? It had been ignored up to this point, but it became evident that it was the question on everyone's mind including my own. I loved my *instant family* dearly, right down to our mentally challenged, but very enthusiastic dog. We decided to try and raise money through sponsorship. It was initially my idea that I would need money for such things as hotels for up to 150 nights, food for said duration, and supplies for nights I would have to rough it. The way I figured it, to do it justly, it would require no less than $19,500. Remember, every bit of food I'd eat would have to be purchased along the way at fast food establishments or as light, non-perishable cargo at a grocery store. Add to that the simple pleasure of not having to sleep in the dirt and having access to a real shower. That would run anywhere from fifty to over one hundred dollars depending on what hotel I made it to that day.

Now the focus was on raising capitol for my share of the bills. Also, we still were living at Harry Monster's house. He would continue to make Alice's life an unstable hell until she found some other place of residence. We set a personal goal of twenty-eight thousand dollars, but represented it as a forty thousand dollar goal on the website. That way we could hope to achieve what we needed even if we fell *short* on the mercury meter. If funding was coming from corporations that were buying future likeness and advertising rights, they would be glad to shell out a measly few thousand each... Wouldn't they?

A sports supplement company whom I had sworn by for years was the first to bite the line. They were located in Miramar, FL, not too far from where I lived. Their products were distributed nationwide at the very least. I was honored, and highly encouraged by my first acquisition. After a lot of e-mails, and a few phone calls I was asked to sign a disclaimer, stating I would not misuse any products granted me by the company. I faxed it back, using my company's resources, along with a list of the products I would like to have for the trip. Weeks later, two separate packages arrived with far more product than I could ever carry in a backpack. I felt like a superstar. Hell, I felt like an athlete, an extreme one at that. The issue of funding, however, remained unsolved.

The next true sponsor had an office in Las Olas, FL, the ritzy business & beach strip in the Ft. Lauderdale area. Their craft was the production and distribution of Tibetan goji berries. The CEO sat down with me more than once at his office. He fronted money for an NPR, or National Press Release, that can still be found by doing a Google search for American Dream Walk, or my name. Please note: the NPR lists a departure date of October 18th. I had to reschedule so as to give myself more time to acquire proper assets. He also set me up with free product, one hundred dollars, and four organic cotton t-shirts baring his company's symbol for me to wear on my journey. It was an amazing accomplishment, one I'm truly grateful for, but where's the whale?

Just recently I took a bus to the CW 34 station in West Palm Beach for an interview. It's supposed to air Sunday, the 21st. Although impoverished and hungry, I still manage to get the media interested in my walk. Maybe all my distractions are gone for a reason. Perhaps the Divine Force is clearing the brush from the path I've volunteered to trek. Hopefully the "impoverished" detail will change, soon. I recently acquired a job. Irony of all ironies, it's at another mortgage company, something I firmly swore I would never do again. I haven't seen the woman I love or the children I'd step in front of a bullet to preserve for far too long. Sometimes a man must do what he must. I'd shovel shit in ninety-degree weather if it meant I was a contributing member of the household. It's too bad *they* weren't hiring. Taco Bell, Popeye's, they won't give me the time of day. Does it seem odd only to me that I got 5 hits on my resume to sell mortgages before a single offer for a lesser skilled profession? Whatever, I don't intend to be there very long. I'll sell a few loans, give all the money to Alice, and just venture out on the American Dream Walk in survival mode. Not *Survivor* mode. Those little douches wouldn't know thing-one about John "Lofty" Wiseman's, nor Bear Grylls' comprehension of "roughing it." After, I'll write a book and maybe someday Alice and I can sit on a beach with the kids, stress free and happy. I'm walking to save my own *American Dream* just as much as I am hoping to inspire others to do the same with theirs'. I don't want to be on the roller coaster called *Sales* anymore. A two-year degree doesn't afford me many options as ascertained by my recent job quest. What's a ninja to do? I feel helpless and I just hope that my fiancé understands. I would walk around the perimeter of the US if I thought it would result in a better life for us. Now I'm gambling on myself, and my passion to be a writer. What better person to place a wager on? It's terrifying and confidence inspiring at once, if that makes sense. I know I either lose big or win big and the only person who is responsible for either outcome holds my impressive apple stem as I pee. Let's clarify; ME. This is a halfway house, not prison. Prisons are much cleaner.

Maybe the world would understand, given the circumstances, if I got angry and pointed the finger elsewhere. I point the finger in the mirror and ask, "What can you learn from this?" I take full responsibility for choosing not to continue my education. I'm not really sure a guy with a mind wired like mine would be happy in *any* profession outside his true passion. It would be the same tug-of-war with higher levels of distraction. Mortgage money was immediate gratification. It's my fault for ignoring the grander picture. If I had known more about life at the time, I may have saved more and spent less. Who doesn't say that to some degree at one point or another in their lives? I refuse to be negative or entertain a moment of self-pity. If I want to feel bad for someone, I need only visit the veterans at the hospital where I go to volunteer unofficially. These brave, old chaps kept the gears of this country greased long enough for me to taste the freedom that I once took for granted. When my time came, I served as well. The time to do so has come again and it's long overdue. Jesus Jones, I'm experiencing an overblown sensation of self-importance. Call a medic!

I shouldn't be this blinded by nobility when I can't even be a man for the ones who mean everything to me. What business do I have walking away from them? In my mind I understand why. It may be difficult to see on the surface. I'm doing this so I have something to give back to them. I believe that this quest to save the American Dream will directly or indirectly lead to something good.

I'm a goddamn poster child for the housing crisis. I not only devoted my professional career to being one who funded the *Dream*, but I also became a casualty of the game. I'm on both sides of this spinning coin as it passes through time and space. I have an opportunity, an obligation, to lead by example. Maybe ancient guilt or regret fuels part of this desire, and now I have a chance to save my own soul. I never hurt families with malicious intent, but I've failed to accomplish refinances for former clients when the rules of lending began to change. Promises I believed were true and solid became as hollow as my stomach is now. A part of me blames myself for everything that doesn't go according to plan. I wasn't even one of the shit bags in this whole mess. I have an honest heart. Let me now demonstrate what it is to be an empowered citizen of this land. You can kick it, but the *Dream* will never stay down. It lives in my core as it does in all of us. It just needs a wake-up call.

I will walk to prove great feats are still possible by any person in this country, even a broken down nobody like myself with a faulty spine and chronic pains. I was born with a low degree of spina bifida, or ill-formed vertebrae. From that I managed to compress three disks in separate areas of my back. They call it a *herniated* disk, but to me that expression is reserved for the elderly. At age seventeen I was told by a specialist that I was well on my way to a very dreadful future. Arthritis, sciatica, and frequent muscle spasms are a part of my life. I usually just ignore it. It was easy to do so with a desk job. There isn't a whole lot of twisting and bending required unless you're the boss's new secretary. I spent one overnight shift as a FedEx employee unloading tractor trailers filled with packages. I was nineteen, and the money would have been ideal. I couldn't repeatedly twist at the waist with any amount of weight in my grasp. I had to accept defeat, and as Clint Eastwood pointed out, know my limitations. I was always able to bench press, do curls, and all that stuff because the back is kept fairly straight. The weight is evenly distributed. Wearing a backpack will pose less of a threat of injury on this walk than say, waking up on cold, hard earth.

People of this generation, my generation, have been brainwashed into accepting defeat well before mustering up any efforts to achieve. We have a lot of ambition, sitting around like the Forum and philosophizing. Starbuck's is a great place to find a high concentration of opinionated seekers. People get all worked up over conversations involving changing the world, and making a difference. They are clever to point out the faults of a system, but rarely provide an alternative idea to replace them. It's like watching children getting all excited to go out and play in the first snowfall. They can't sit still; eyes are wide, as they're released into the yard. As soon as the first bitter chill penetrates their jackets, they're running back inside. They were certain they wanted something until they felt the first creeping sensation of discomfort. What good is ambition without the courage to stay in the game once action is taken? If you believe in something, shouldn't you deal with the unpleasant byproducts resulting from standing your ground? *Adversity* hasn't had a challenging workout in some time. It went from mass building exercises during the forming years of our country, continued that regiment until about the end of the second World War, and today it's barely breaking a sweat with it's 20 minutes here and there on a treadmill. We rarely get to a point where we even see its face. I'd rather be remembered as that lunatic who went on an insanely long walk than be categorized as another statistic of the "What If…" Generation. I don't want to wonder what could have been. I want to be in a constant state of movement, change, and self-evolution.

There is plenty of Wisdom out there to be absorbed. It would take many lifetimes before I got bored with the quest. I truly have nothing in common, nor do I understand those who'd rather ignore the whole thing all together. They box themselves in with as many constraints and distractions as possible so they never have time to think about what they're missing. This is at the core of why many people hate their jobs, get divorced, and otherwise live in misery. Their instinct for adventure can be diluted, but can never truly be absent. Some particle of it, however small, always remains. That idea that they were meant for something greater gets stomped down pretty hard by tradition, society, what the media tells us to do, police, and the government. It was all your head knew when you were a child, however. If you wanted to be a giraffe, there was nothing you needed to concern yourself with. You never doubted that you could be one. Fast forward twenty or thirty years. What happened to that limitless wonder and excitement? Where did the passion for living go? Why are you in a cubical staring at a computer screen and not outside jumping in mud puddles? Do you want to wake up one day and find you've run out of time for all of the things you've been putting off until the moment was *right*? Things will never be perfect in career, in family, in whatever. Stop waiting for a magical moment that will never come and charge out into the unknown for a while. Just don't run back inside too fast if you get cold.

I'm officially petitioning each and every one of you to grab yourselves by your ears and yank yourselves from the rut we, as a nation, are in. No one is stopping us from becoming what we've always wanted except ourselves. Defeat that, and the rest is easy.

I'm more proud of my country at a time like this when the chips are down. It shows the true virtue of our humanity and vulnerability. It creates opportunity for us to change what we don't like, and what is no longer working for us. It carries with it the responsibility to take the necessary *steps* for improvement. I can't speak for anyone else, but I've got a lot more fights left in me.

My pen is almost out of ink. I was going off on a tangent. My story turned into a speech, a monologue. I always seem to win at the one-man argument.

Should I be focused more at the surface of things, at my current status and interactions? Maybe, but I'm afraid of it. I'm putting all my effort into effecting change for myself, but I need to be careful where I lay my trust. If one career can result in this much loss, how can I know what other solutions will lead to the same troubles later? The more complex the career, the more time and energy must be invested. I'd hate to assume I was doing the right thing only to later find out I had been had, once again. I'm not particularly special. My brain is no gem to be sought after for scientific experimentation. My rejection of tradition and my mistrust of commonly held values can be a virtue at times, because it makes me think for myself. Unfortunately, it's not always advantageous to be seen as a *free spirit*. People are cautious when they sense my unrest. Employers don't want a loose cannon, or someone who will challenge their authority. I am aware of all of this, but I can't do anything about it. If I could change, I'd only be pretending to change, and no one can lie to himself or herself forever. I've tried, failed, and as a result, lashed out with even stronger convictions than before.

Soon, the church doors will open up the road. I'm told I can get a prepared breakfast in a to-go box there. Someday I'll come back to these places and donate my time serving food to others. All I have time for right now is volunteering at the VA on Sundays. I'm no longer enrolled in the chef school. There I fed the homeless three times a day. With the new mortgage nonsense I'm tangled up in, the times would conflict. I have yet to master being in two places at once, and I need the job. I wonder what a

Baptist eats? Likely it's something dipped, or perhaps boiled, in water.

Everybody Knows

I borrowed the title for this section from a Leonard Cohen song.
Sorry Leonard. I hope you don't mind.

Part I: Bad Mamba Jamba

September 22nd, 2008

 I was almost stabbed today. I know *almost* doesn't put one at the edge of their seat, but it was quite an intense episode from the firsthand perspective. Having scored my first check the previous day, I finally had some food to cook. While tending the stove, I was engaged in a rare, light-hearted conversation with a fellow inmate of this horrific establishment.   There was a third party, my latest prison reject for a roommate, standing beside me at the sink. He was hacking away at a coconut with some sort of cutting device, making a lot of dramatic actions with his hand. It was obvious he wanted to draw our attention. When dealing with ex-cons, they normally still have a mindset of someone inside. There everything is a purposeful gesture meant to intimidate those around them. It's both a defensive and offensive survival strategy. Earlier this new roommate had been caught stealing pink lemonade mix from another. Instead of eliminating the problem, management decided to move the guy who was victimized by the theft to a different wing.
 The gentleman I was conferring with was leaning against the wall behind me. He was the only person I ever took initiative to talk to since I arrived here. Unlike the other thirty or so mutants inside these walls, he was here for similar reasons as I: Bad luck, and in his case, an addict wife who influenced him to take the apple from the tree and taste it.
Before he spiraled out of control himself, he was a high school teacher. Deductive reasoning would lead one to the conclusion that his level of formal education was not only above my own,

which is no great feat, but galaxies away from the rest of these freaks.

As he did often, the man with the coconut and Don King hairstyle was talking to himself incoherently and giggling as he did it. It was the type of habit you'd normally see from a patient in a mental ward. He made even the more hardened ex-cons nervous with his actions. Just being from Pahokee was no excuse for this level of lunacy. I don't think spending time in the Glades facility helped matters much.

My acquaintance, for the lack of a better word, and I were joking back and forth uttering quotes from various Monty Python sketches. While I was being given the "Spam" lecture, I noticed my bread was tied in a way I would never leave it. I made the comment, "I'd like to know why I always come back here to find less food than when I left." I'm not petty, but I had lived off nothing but bread and water for the past three dragging weeks. Now that I finally had food, I was going to protect it.

"Don Coconut" had a massive upper body, likely due in part to many days spent in the *yard*. For a short guy he was still a force to be reckoned with. He began stabbing the countertop with all his mite. "You motherfucker," he growled, "I'm gonna beat your ass, you fuck! Come at me talkin' 'bout some fuckin' bread?"

"Did I say anything about *you*?" I quickly replied in an engaging tone.

"Who the fuck else is here? You fuckin' piece of shit! I pay to live here if I want something, I'll fuckin' take it. It'd be different if it was a pair of socks!"

"Oh, so that would be crossing the line, but everything else is fair game? If I notice I'm being robbed I'm going to say something about it," I said in a tone uncharacteristically calm for the situation.

By now he was an inch from my nose. This was the first time I realized I wasn't the shortest guy living here. He said something about cutting my head off and eating my ears first as he clenched ever tighter on the weapon in his right hand. His arms were at his sides for the time being, but I knew I was in real, possibly immediate danger.

"If I had any doubt before, I guess you solved the bread mystery for me now." What the hell did I say that for? Was I trying to get killed in this kitchen? What would ever become of my uneaten Spam?

There isn't much you can say to someone incapable of rational thought. My acquaintance attempted to redirect the focus. "Hey man, you don't want to get thrown…" That was all he got out before Don Coconut made a lateral movement and was in his face, this time holding the knife chest-level.

"Who fuckin' asked you? I don't give a fuck! Do I look like someone who fuckin' cares, motherfucker?" There were a lot of other profanities spewing forth from his heavily bearded face. Don had an Afro that started three feet above his scalp and didn't end for a foot below his chin. I don't think he could cut it because it had been declared the natural habitat of an endangered bird, the last of its kind.

With the pressure off me, I left my friend there to deal with Don and I sought help from the manager. I paused in front of the television, but it was difficult to concentrate on Deep Space 9. All that bloodcurdling racket coming from the man about to carve up another was getting on my nerves. When someone does something, but they don't really *do* anything, what is that called? It's not *state worker*. That was my guess, too… The manager, we'll call him Robert, because that's his name. He came on the scene and asked Don to take his coconut and go for a walk. Wow, Robert. What would we have done without you?

Two men almost becoming chalk outlines in Robert's kitchen and the possibility that canned meat would go to waste only prompted him to break up the situation, not call the cops. I don't know how much more I can take of this shit. Luckily Don came back later and acted up again, this time with Robert. I witnessed the argument going on in the tiny little office off the kitchen. Don was sent on his way this evening, which is fortunate for me because I now have a lower risk of being murdered while I sleep.

"So I've got that going for me, which is nice."

-Bill Murray,
Caddy Shack

Part II: Barrier

September 24th, 2008

I see a lot of people falling short of their full potential. I do not want to live beneath mine, real or assumed. There is a scene in my aforementioned screenplay dealing with the same principles that motivate my proposed hike. In, "Logos: A Mock Epic" there is a young man writing a story, on his desktop computer, titled *Message Into Space*. It deals with shyness and fear. The backdrop is that of a college lecture hall with the wise, aging professor delivering a monologue that can best be described as a call to action.

He explains that those of us who choose to ignore, or otherwise waste, our given talents and strengths are the epitome of evil men. We were meant to use these gifts to enhance the world around us. Bluntly put in the professor's terms, "Best intentions are useless thoughts. They are devices of idle people." He continues, "When the light illuminating our planet reaches the eyes of distant life, it carries with it our voice, our message into space. These pacifying *best intentions* are never seen if not acted out. Those who philosophize more than they act are misrepresenting themselves before the entire universe, and beyond. Your best qualities should never be your best-kept secrets. It is a selfish fool who does so."

Every morning I look in the mirror and ask myself if I'm doing everything I should be, if I'm being true to my gut feeling. Am I taking initiative and pursuing what I believe is the correct path? Am I a man in motion, or am I frozen in time? Normally I ask these questions in thought versus aloud. I don't want to be viewed as another Don Coconut.

The fact that I can write these words and that you, the reader, can digest them means we are still alive. If we aren't doing what we should be there's still time for us to change that. When it comes to any feeling of unrest, any itch, it is there for a reason. It's a result of our attempts to starve and kill a part of ourselves. Maybe we learned it was more trouble than it was worth, or it was too grand of an idea to ever be fully realized. Addicts feel the same sensation when coming down from their high. With the drug no longer saturating their cells, the cells cry out like babies for another bottle. If it a dream or a goal, why the hell would we want it gone? Were we convinced it was invalid? By whom? What credentials did these people possess to grant them such power and influence over our actions?

I know my greatest barrier and it is thy self! That's why I was able to put all my effort into writing a screenplay, but had made few people aware of its existence. I chickened out, and convinced myself it was impossible for me to succeed. That's honesty. I can't continue to lie to myself about it and hope to get any further in my personal evolution. I could envision being a Hollywood filmmaker, but the whole thing was too good for me. The idea that dreams come true was too much for me to comprehend. There was no wall between myself and success, less the one I created with my own two hands. Better late than never to come to terms with this and press forward.

Pretty soon I'll be on this walk. It may have to come earlier than planned. I am still behind on rent here and the pressure is increasing. I'd sooner leave than be thrown out. The way I look at it, if I do right by Alice and give her money for our storage fees, that will leave me short of what was asked for by October 3rd, Friday. I would rather give her the money than Robert. That means I'll have to adjust my plans from October 18th to Sunday, October 5th. There's no chance I'll be closing a loan with this company. I have taken a lot more applications by phone than the guys around me, but it's all for naught. What good is getting someone involved in refinancing if there's no loan to offer them? I scrapped almost thirty applications of the forty-two I've drafted. The other option, loan modification, is an evil practice when *negotiated* by a third party. We're asked to get a check for no less than 4% of the client's loan balance before processing the application. At that point our imaginary team of skilled lawyers are supposedly hammering on the client's mortgage holder. The lawyers, with the client's best interest in their hearts of course, will then strong-arm the bankers into reducing the rate and improving the conditions of the loan. The result is meant to be a more affordable monthly payment for the client whom otherwise does not qualify for a refinance program. For the company I work for, the average obtainable savings is roughly seventy-five dollars. Compare that to the $8,000 shelled out by the client for a loan size of say, $200,000. They have to be behind in their payments for them to qualify, so where do you think they got this money? Likely, you as a mortgage consultant just robbed the clients' children of their college funds, or forced the hapless souls to prematurely crack their 401K accounts. Most families need a lot more help than a lousy seventy-five dollars per month. Facing the loss of their house, these families desperately agree to this horrible plan. They think if they spend less here, and go without that, maybe, just maybe their kids will have a place to sleep at night.

What type of monster can kick a family while they're down? They're taking one last fee before the inevitable foreclosure. Instead of fearing the federal government or feeling ashamed for creating this mess, the companies are finding new ways to be evil. This is the sort of practice encouraged by my new bosses. As George Clooney said in *From Dusk 'til Dawn*, "I may be an asshole, but I'm not a *fucking* asshole." If I could bring myself to do this I could easily fix a lot of what's broken for myself, financially. I could have something to contribute to Alice and the children. It would all be blood money, however, watermarked with tears of other people's sorrow. Once a step is taken down that path there is no turning back.

My base check is petty. If broken down hourly it only comes out to be $7.50. I'm spinning my wheels in a position I have no more business being in. I've seen the end of my career. I was weeded out through the process of natural selection. For others in that line of work, they too are an endangered species for the time being. I don't foresee them remaining at that status level for long. Most will survive the drought by selling their souls and practicing like my example. When the good times come back I will not be rushing in the door with hungry eyes and a fresh resume in hand. I'll likely be working at a fast food restaurant and planning my next big idea. Whether I like it or not, I must change just as the details and conditions of my situation have. It is my responsibility to grow from this, to adapt, and to absorb everything I possibly can. I've already learned to change my attitude about career types. What I once saw as the professional and noble, I know to be undignified and rotten. What I saw as high school dork work I no longer do. I do not frown on the people, or their reasons, for showing up to work everyday making an effort for themselves and for their families. The concept that any gainful, honest employment is good employment has sunken in. My attitude and view is more mature than it was when I was a young punk. Now I'm an older punk. What a difference!

I have no money for this little hop, skip, and jump to the West Coast. Whatever I need I will have to find using survival tactics, resourcefulness, and adaptability. I'm left-handed, so I can't lose. I know I'll be watched over from above and so long as I never develop a negative attitude. Good things will happen when I need them to. Mark my words, my greatest sponsor is the one that's with us all whether we choose to acknowledge Him or not. God Himself is left-handed. That is why the Son is seated at the right hand of the Father—so they don't fight over the armrest.

Part III: Whatever happened to *forever*?

If you leave now, you won't be here... A sinking ship gathers no moss... I read the book from cover to cover. Tomorrow I'll read the part in between... I thought 'twelve step' referred to some sort of dance lesson... Intuition vs. logic in a steel cage match... It takes two, baby. Fuck this! I hate math... I'll tell you 'what,' but I'd rather just answer the question... Lucky for me, Friday was weeks away... I have half a mind to tell your mother. The other half is for tying my shoes... There are two kinds of people in this world. Where's the remote?

September 25th, 2008

It is a somber evening in the life of your trusted narrator. At least I think it is. I'm not really sure what "somber" means. Around four-thirty this afternoon, the tension between Alice and I boiled over. She broke off our engagement over the telephone. I am still too angry to feel the full impact of my loss, but it's coming. Once I have time to realize, as I usually do, that *I'm* the asshole in the situation, then the panic and anxiety will not creep in. It will kick the doors of my ignorance off their fucking hinges. I had good reason to feel hurt and upset. My mistake that I seem doomed to repeat, is that I express sorrow as anger and hostility. If one resorts to screaming, they've already lost the battle. Nothing said after that is validated. Even if I'm right in thinking, I'm wrong by behavior. Hindsight is a dirty whore.

If I am left alone with my thoughts tonight the only book I'll be writing will be forcibly called, "Lunatic Chronicles," with a publishing address of a local mental facility. I need a strong distraction immediately. My heart is emptier than a Michael Bay joint. No amount of professional achievement can compete with the love of a good woman. They say everybody is someone else's fool. I proved that when I drove away the one virtue left in my life. I'm so ashamed of myself for what I've become. I've been lashing out at those who matter most to me because I don't want to drag them down in this misery. When I have misery it's too miserable to even want to entertain company. Pride, vanity, whatever...

My scale is imbalanced. On one side I have this epic adventure planned, and on the other, I'm staring boarding house eviction in the eye, have no money for Alice, and I was robbed of $176 last night! That was money intended for her for my half of the storage expenses.

I was doing some running around in town on the metro system. I wasn't aware that the last Palm Tran number 1 bus doesn't make a full route. It stopped in Lake Worth, ten or so miles short of my destination. If I wanted to get back to the boarding house, I'd have to walk from there. There is a curfew of eleven o'clock that I was bound to be late for whether I be Daniel Urbaetis or Jesse Owens. It was aggravating, but I chalked it up to simple rationale. I needed some exercise for the big walk, anyway. I stepped into a convenience store and purchased three 24-ounce Miller Lite beer cans. With that I took a plastic soda cup to pour them in. Now, having disguised my means of release, I walked confidently down the street, US 1. It was long into my travels before I hit the unsavory areas. There was really no avoiding them by foot. My boarding house was located in the epicenter of an expansive ghetto. With previous experience consorting with hustlers under my belt from my mortgage days, the wisdom I gained from my current living conditions, and a considerable amount of liquid courage, I went headlong into danger. I was only three blocks from the finish line when it happened.

Vagrants occupy the areas where free food can be found. In great numbers, they camp out on ratty, military issued, woolen blankets near churches and missions. There was one up ahead called St. Anne's. If I was going to run into any disturbance along this road, I knew it would be there. The scene looked less like a US city and more like a third world country. It reminded me of my travels to Mazatlan, Mexico while aboard the Coast Guard Cutter, Alert. It didn't take long before I found myself warding off requests for change and cigarettes. In a situation like this, it's best to walk tall, confident, and poised. Introduce a swagger into the step and appear to belong there. Keep looking ahead, and only if necessary, verbalize rejection to their begging. Don't stop walking. There's no telling what is waiting for, or what may catch up with, you. Be suspicious of everyone. It's the only way to prevent falling victim to scams and setups. Even then there is still great risk. Unfortunately I had to walk through the middle of a group of four consisting of a fat, transvestite prostitute, a malnourished chap with hyperactivity, a regular, old-fashioned prostitute, and another man dripping with repugnant sweat. I was the only macadamia nut in this candy bar. Just another night in paradise…

Everything got quiet as I approached. All eyes were on me. Then, the hyper guy spoke. He stood in my path and asked me ridiculous questions like, "Hey brotha, what time you got," and "You gotta cigarette, or change for the bus?" What fucking bus? There wouldn't be transit authority on this road for seven hours. Maybe he had a busy day ahead, full of mergers and acquisitions, but I had my suspicions to the contrary. That's when I felt the impact. I was intentionally bumped into by one of the other three. Having seen *My Blue Heaven*, I knew I just got picked. Immediately, I checked for my wallet in my back pocket. It was gone. My aunt, who is no longer with us, gave me that wallet years ago before she was diagnosed with leukemia. I was in rage. I was ready to beat all four to death with my bare hands. Well, maybe not the repugnant guy, but I'd find a two-by-four or something for him. As I looked them over with eyes ablaze, I noticed the transvestite was walking briskly down a side street. She… *It* had my money already drawn out and clenched in one hand. The wallet was in the other. *It* threw my wallet over its shoulder and got into a beat up, little red car from the passenger side. There was no traffic at this hour so the getaway was fluid. I ran over and picked up my possession and examined it for remains. All was there but the cash. By the time I looked up, Hyper Guy was standing behind me. I turned to face him as he spoke in an apologetic tone, "You can forget about that change, now." I fantasized ripping his head off with my bare hands like the Predator. Instead, I continued on my walk. The doors to the boarding house got locked at curfew and did not reopen until nine in the morning. The policy stated that if a resident is out for the night they could not return to their room right away. First they'd have to urinate in a plastic cup for substance testing purposes. Can't wait. I slept on the concrete landscaping flush to the building. At least it wasn't cold or raining.

Coming fresh from an event like this I was in no mood to be passive or understanding with Alice. I was incapable of listening. I have been sharing only some of the horror stories of this life with her. I hesitate to say too much. She has her own mess to deal with being under the fascist control of Harry Monster, and having to work to provide for her kids. The last thing she needs to worry about is myself. The woman balances enough stress without mine sprinkled like poisonous cinnamon on top. I try to talk about my occasional visits to the beaches of Singer Island, and how I body surf the most intimidating waves I can catch. She probably thinks I am a beach bum rather than a guy who got up at five in the morning and filled out as many applications, shook as many hands, and provided as many resumes as he could. I did that everyday until malnourishment would weaken me to the point where I had to return to these confines.

I know, or at least I want to believe, that she still loves me. Lately, it seemed she had a callous, unfeeling aura about her that came through in her voice tone and in the words she chose. Words like "dude" and "man" are reserved for people who are more distant from your heart. They aren't to be executed in conversations with your true love. It tore me apart and drove me mad every time she'd use them. I was getting incredibly uncomfortable vibes from her. If I had food, I would have thrown it up. I thought perhaps she was seeing another. How would I ever know? Sixty or so miles may as well have been a thousand with no means of travel on my part. It took four buses and just as many hours to get within proximity of Harry's home. I traveled it one time, secretly showing up for a kiss and a stripped down supply of personal effects. Alice did the kissing, not Harry. I never thought that driveway would be the scene of our last tender moment together. Is this really the end? It's difficult to say. Too many things happen in the mind to trust one's own conclusions at times.

I've made my mistakes, but Alice made her share, too. Some were outright unbelievable and haunted me throughout our relationship. Even now as I replay every moment we spent together, I wonder if I was *under the ether*. Was I not seeing something I should have all along? A man could go crazy with such thoughts. I'm too vulnerable at the moment to be trying to make sense of things. I'll make connections to actions and events that aren't really connected until the picture I hypothesize becomes too real to ignore. I'll wonder, "Why didn't I see this before?" I'll believe, "I've been lied to from the beginning."

For now, since I can't avoid thinking about it, I need to stick to basics. She could have been more supportive emotionally, and I could have listened more. I could have shared more, although I was under the impression that certain things boil down to small talk. I'm not the type to waste my time with it. I want to jump out the top of my skull and run like the wind when I'm being subjected to someone else's irrelevant, mindless banter. Does wind actually "run?" I'm no scientist, but I suspect this is an inaccurate cliché. I don't care about anyone's opinion on how I choose to carryout my day, so why would I recap every monotonous detail of it? There's bound to be a commentary.

Shock and denial are my two best friends helping soften the blow, presently. Soon, they will be on their way to help others like myself, leaving me to deal with the emotions without a filter. I wanted us to stop fighting, but not like this. I never for a moment thought Alice and I would not be together *forever*. It reminds me of the final episode of *Cheers*. Norm, played by George Wendt, knew Sam Malone would come back to the bar. "You can never betray your true love." Maybe I'm like that. If it wasn't Alice, maybe writing is the true love that I can never betray. It should be noted I that I warned this was a bad time to be having these thoughts.

I was hoping for more of a Christian Slater, Patricia Arquette ending like in *True Romance*. That was Tarantino screenwriting at its finest. Love in a world gone mad and the two of us against it… Somehow we'd survive it because we had each other. Now I am alone, and I miss my baby.

Preparation

The Birth of the Punk Rock Nomad

"I got a lot of people telling me I'm outta my mind, and I don't know why..."

-Tim Armstrong of Rancid

October 3rd, 2008

In the beginning I walked 2.94 miles every morning from my bus stop on Griffin Road to work at the mortgage company. This was back in the months when I was still living in Harry Monster's suburban cave dwelling. After work I'd walk another 2.94 miles back to catch the $1.25 ride. If you haven't already seen it, that's the route I'm walking in the CBS 4 news piece. In it, they compare my walk to the run executed by America's favorite retard. I'm not referring to Dane Cook, although he *is* a mongoloid. I mean the one played by the great Tom Hanks, *Forrest Gump*. They went so far as to show a clip from the film.

Up until two mornings ago, weather permitting, I would speed walk for a total of 9.8 miles roundtrip. Yes, from an outsider's point of view, it looks as queer as it sounds. It was a necessary part of my conditioning and endurance training. I'm not a lifer with any admiration for the exercise. By this time I had acquired a cheaply made pocketknife in case I *ran* into trouble en route.

Earlier, I mentioned one of my sponsors is a supplement company. I have been drinking energy elixirs, daily. Really, I'm just trying to get rid of the bulk of them. There's no way a man under 125 pounds could lug all that freight on his back for any given distance. The other sponsor, the goji berry distributor, promised a small stipend that I will use for food and survival necessities along the way. A certain famous submarine sandwich company gave me $100 in coupons to use at any of their locations. That should get me down the block. Like everything else it will have to be rationed. I didn't end up with anything near the coverage I was hoping for regarding corporate involvement. If it worked out my way, Apple would have donated an I-Pod so I didn't go mad with boredom or loneliness, Red Bull would have sent along a spotter who could have followed along with me and kept me buzzed, AT&T would have provided a phone with GPS capability, the Discovery Channel would have sent a small film crew along to make the documentary, UPS would have donated mailbox drop points along my path at their satellite retail locations, Oprah would have given me some couch time, Ellen would have done the same, and so would have Craig Fergusen. Not like I had high expectations or anything. If anyone else attempts this, please be sure to at least get Conan O'Brien's attention, or David Letterman's if you're slumming it.

As for the technical aspects, there's a lot to take into consideration if one's aim is to succeed, or at the very least, not die.

- I have to seal all of my clothing and delicate supplies in large, plastic storage bags. They look like the type used for freezing leftovers. This is done in an effort to protect items from weather damage. It will prevent potential leaks in supplies like toothpaste, soap gel, and other liquids and powders from contaminating the whole bag. Also, dirty clothing can be sealed in separate bags so as to not spread any soil or odor onto fresh apparel. A healthy backpack is the number one priority. I will be depending on what's inside of it for the duration.

- I've said this before, but instead of mapping the shortest route, I must plot according to the most walker-friendly conditions. I don't need to draw unwanted attention from authorities. Especially since I'll have no money and no true place of residence to disclose if questioned. I'll be a prime target for an arrest for vagrancy. I plan to approach police officers and engage them in conversation first. I'll have the website for them to reference to prove my story. I've also acquired simple business cards with the web address on them to hand out not only to officials, but to whomever I feel would take the time to visit my site.

- Another task while plotting is the consideration of drawbridges and other forms of passage that may have no sidewalk or shoulder. I don't want to walk myself into a dead end, thereby losing valuable time and unnecessarily exhausting supplies or energy.
- I have been mentally preparing myself for this undertaking as well. I'll eventually be faced with unfavorable hiking conditions, such as rough, overgrown terrain and brutal weather. I'm going to be very close to speeding traffic in addition. I'm roughing it, so I'm not going to be afforded the luxury of hotels nor of proper bathing facilities. I'll be *scrub-showering* in bathrooms as I go. That will be the most difficult for me to conquer. When it comes to hygiene I am obsessive. I put deodorant on after taking off a jacket in fear that the movement of one material over another may have degraded the initial application. Someone must have told me I smelled as a little kid or something because I am a devout follower of sanitation in every aspect. I don't mind getting dirty. In fact that's fun. I just don't want to be grimy, greasy or otherwise disgusting.
- Let's be honest. I just lost the support of the woman I love. If there's any assumption out there that this recent event doesn't affect my psyche, squash it now. I'd be losing more of her if I let go. I will not let hope that I can somehow make things right between Alice and myself die. This is my work, but she is my life. I'll be missing all my loved ones and fearing loss of even more support. This must all be boiled down or ironed out before the big day. Strengths of the body *and* of the mind are necessary for this to be a successful venture.

And I get to do it all with an enormous green monkey on my back...

Yesterday I sent an e-mail to my boss and a few select co-workers thanking them for the experience. I told them I was not a good fit and that I regretted not giving them more notice, but that I was departing. After sending the e-mail I got up and walked out the door to the elevator. Seven floors down, a short walk through the atrium, and then fresh air. I left around eleven in the morning. It was a beautiful day. Instead of taking a bus anywhere, I decided I'd walk to the VA Medical Center, four miles away, and say goodbye to some of the people I had grown attached to. I met a lot of respectable men while teaching them how to use the computers in their recreation room. As I was walking I felt a rush of warmth come over me and I couldn't help but grin. I was really doing it. There was no going back, now. I had set the wheels in motion. Whether this adventure even remotely resembles the actions of a sane individual I don't know. It's not a debate I'm even slightly interested in. I'm impressed with myself for having the balls to follow a plan that has required so much strength in my own convictions. I stayed true to my beliefs in the face of that *Adversity* fellow I mentioned. I had no one else's support. Last I spoke with Alice, she called me a homeless loser with no future. That's love, dear friends. My parents are good people who know me best and they don't understand why I would do this. What a paradox! It's me against the world in an effort to save it. I didn't pay my rent today. I have to leave by this evening. I have little under $130 for the trip. The goal was to raise $28,000. That's like burying yourself in the mat rather than clearing the bar in a pole vault.

I'll walk the three or so miles to Singer Island this morning and enjoy the waves one last time. Then I'll gather whatever will fit in the bag, leave the rest behind, and take a bus to my starting point, Commercial Blvd, in Lauderhill—just outside of Tamarac, FL. I'll be going south on the ride just to come back this way on foot. I said I was starting in Tamarac, so that's where I'm starting. Even if it *is* sixty something miles away, I am a man of my word. The first thing I'm donating to the center will be all of my professional work clothes. I won't need them where I'm heading. I'm calling all the shots from this day forth. The anticipation of change, of adventure, of freedom excites me. I wonder where I'll sleep tonight, tomorrow night...

One Final Kick in the Nuts

Evening of October 3rd, 2008

     I do not have sufficient time to write much with the current, imposing demands on me. I need to be sure to catch the bus out of here and still allot myself time for the other two connecting routes. After a quick survey of weight versus practical use versus available space, the inventory of my belongings is going to have to be cut down quite dramatically. I've made some difficult choices when it came to my clothing. I cut it down to five full sets, an additional sweater, and extra boxers and socks. OK, so maybe I have a few t-shirts more than I'm letting on, but they are some of my favorite. I'll be damned if I'm to part with my Dropkick Murphys shirt, my Bruce Lee, or my Operation Ivy.

     I had four books I wanted to bring, but I narrowed it down to only the one, Jack Foster's *How to Get Ideas*. I discovered it in the library at the VA hospital during my official stay. It gave me something to do in between favored Discovery Channel programs. I've always believed books found a person at that perfect moment when it would make the greatest impact on their lives. This book was confidence inspiring and helped me salvage my optimism.

     I tried calling Alice again, but that was a mistake. There were no positive words to be had, but at least I got to hear her voice once more. Mick Jagger sang, "You can't always get what you want… But if you try sometimes you might find, you get what you need." Sadly however, I'm left with little hope of a reunion after listening to her hostile tone and negative opinion. She's very hurt and I only have myself to blame for how I'm feeling presently. I wanted to see her before I departed tomorrow, but she didn't want anything to do with the idea. I feel like my heart has died. I'm nauseous, dizzied. I've been running around in an angered frenzy. Anxiety is at a record high. I have been desperately trying to focus on the task at hand, but to no avail. That's what inspired me to sit down for a moment with my pen and notebook. This is my therapy. It's the only kind I can afford, and it's probably the best there is for me. I can't be too out of control physically, if I'm releasing my emotions onto paper.

Onto less important topics... I learned that the news crew that ran the initial story on CBS 4, will not be available for a follow-up Sunday. I can't linger around in the same area. I have to be in motion. None of my sponsors will be present, nor do I have any faith in them keeping their promises once I'm gone. With or without anyone in this world giving a shit, I will be leaving from the Super Target at 12:30 PM. I'll buy some cheap survival items from their camping department, fire down some energy drinks, and be on my way, rain or shine. With a bit of luck I'll manage to forego food all together, and modify my metabolism to run purely on beer and liquor. If I were my normal self, this Alice situation would clearly demand it.

Oh, Sailor Jerry, where are you? I could use your *92 Proof Wisdom* right now...

Infamous Hiking Journal

Compiled from a series of notebook scribbling, this is the daily account of my experiences on the road. Whenever I made it to a library, I'd update my "Web-Tracker" page with whatever days I was backlogged, as separate entries, using the notes and my memory as resources. Computer access is timed and limited. I found myself having to sacrifice large portions of data, and summarize some events unjustly. This is the first time the "Divided Highway" field notes have ever been portrayed as they were intended—in their entirety.

Giovanni Luciano Urbaetis, the GLU that holds us together… The Tomb of the Unknown Porn Star… A man can sleep anywhere… Blister poppin' daddy… What would Bear Grylls do..? Next rest stop, 2,402 miles… Rain, rain, go to Hell… The loss of all support…I'm like the Unabomber, only without the political agenda or math skills… Getting better every moment… Library lounge act… Thanks for the free food… Jesus Jones..! White man make flame… The Punk Rock Nomad Strikes Again… Feeling the flow… Ocala needs a glue factory… Is there a Wal*Mart nearby..? Step away from the chicken… The power struggle for a human soul… How the fuck did I get to Houston, and how the fuck do I get out..? Crazy Ron & the Red Ranger… Wrong Way..! Telemundo…What a ride… Mesa means table… Path to enlightenment… Devil grass blues… Peyote doesn't grow on trees… Desert survival and the woes of martyrdom…

"Just because you're paranoid don't mean they're not after you…"
                                                -Nirvana, *Territorial Pissings*

"How ever far away… Whatever words I say, I will always love you…"

                                                -The Cure, 311 *Love Song*

"You gotta walk like a champion, talk like a champion…"

-Buju Banton, *Champion*

"I've seen the future, brother, it is murder…"

-Leonard Cohen, *The Future*

"Now my guns are blazin, pick it back up and start it all over again…"

-Rancid, *Bloodclot*

"All I know is that I don't know nothing…"

-Operation Ivy, *Knowledge*

"The vision is a new world order…"

-Rancid, *Life Won't Wait*

"Well the hard times come and the hard times go, but I say come one, come all…"

-Rancid, *Hooligans*

"Yeah he's a different color, but we're the same kid,
I'll treat him like my brother, he'll treat me like his…"

-Rancid, *Avenues and Alleyways*

"As if I should care… As if you are listening out there…"

-Mr. Bungle, *Slowly Growing Deaf*

"We reach for an outside point of view, but it's out of touch with me and you
I feel I'm walking into suicide, but you'll be right there by my side
To beam my message into space as I die…"

-Mr. Bungle, *Merry Go Bye-Bye*

"And I didn't trust him because he smiled at me first
Just like the wolf before he bites me…"

-Rancid, *The Wolf*

"It ain't no good when you're misunderstood
When you're rottin' in jail, or wish you would be
Out on the streets like Robin Hood…"

-Rancid, *Coppers*

"I'm free as I stare at the sea…"

-311, *Do You Right*

"He's got a head full of ideas… That you wouldn't believe
…so many tricks up his sleeve… You might think he's a jester
Because he'll make you laugh when you cry
No one else better come for you, best him, test him
Unless (they're) ready to die…"

-311, *You Wouldn't Believe*

"Can't stop the spirits when they need you
This life is more than just a read-through…"

-Red Hot Chili Peppers, *Can't Stop*

"I will never follow you, I will never bother you…
Things have never been so swell, I have never felt this well…"

-Nirvana, *You Know You're Right*

"And when your feverish thoughts are broken
Keep on dreamin' boy, 'cuz when you stop dreamin' it's time to
die…"

-Blind Melon, *Change*

Day 1: "And oh, as I fade away they'll all look at me and say, 'Hey look at him and where he is these days,' When life is hard you have to change..." It was as expected, being the first day. My backpack is far too heavy for sensible travel. I know it will take me days of difficult decisions to discard the unnecessary. Rain came as foretold by the local meteorologists, but it only hung around until midday. I acquired a bicycle chain and a padlock to secure my oversized bag to trees, bike racks, poles, or whatever. This way I don't have to raise as many eyebrows by walking into consumer outlets with it on. It can stand guard outside and act as my lookout. My Big Green Monkey is my only entourage on this trip, so we must make true efforts to get along. In time, I hope my kindness and charm will win it over. Then we can comfortably relax and call one another friends. It *is* my "Wilson." Tom Hanks had a volleyball, and I have my monkey.

There were no media, no sponsors, and no individuals to wish me luck. All I had as comfort was the gray sky, and the acquisition of needed fire-starting supplies along with rain ponchos, cheap thermal blankets, etc. I was as prepared as I could be for the moment. I'd learn the rest through my daily experiences as to what I have too much of and what I lack. Only then will I have a firm comprehension of what is important. I left at 12:35pm from the entrance of Target.

The course is planned as such. I will be walking Commercial Blvd, taking a few, short twists and turns until I get to State Road 7, also known as 441, and heading north. Once in Margate, I will travel east on Sample Road until I get to Military Trail. From there I will again head north. I chose this route because I felt it suiting to walk Military Trail being a veteran, acknowledging the symbolism and meaning behind the walk, and because of my appreciation for the men and women who make sacrifices for our freedom. The VA Medical Center that I spent time at is on this road, many miles north. This will also be a safer path. If I busted down US 1 I'd run right back into the territory where I was robbed that infamous night. I'll be close enough to the ghetto to hear a gunshot's echo, but not close enough to smell it. After I get passed that portion of US 1, I'll cut east and join up with it. It stretches all the way to Maine, and will be ideal for a man who appreciates a consistent path.

I weighed the Big Green Monkey at the first Publix I came to. It's 55 pounds, or 45% of my bodyweight. This is excessive. Measures must be taken immediately. I find bus stop benches very convenient in times like these. I can drop my bag down without having to set it all the way on the ground, providing less of a struggle when putting it back on. The shoulder straps are digging into my flesh and I've already developed a fiery rash of two band marks where they make contact. It's the weight. Today is a day for ironing out the kinks. Speaking of bus stops, many of them are domed with benches, so I was able to get my sleep in one last night. This morning, I simply woke up and got on the bus needed to get me closest to my starting point at the Target.

Stay positive. This is going to be great. The skies have cleared up and the sun is going help keep my tan remain nice and dark. Switch into the tank top and press forward...

Day 2: Today went much better. I find it's easier to walk in the evenings and throughout the night rather than sweat it out in the sun. That has it merits, too because when the sun is shining spirits are high. I'm going to go easy until about 4:30 pm, then increase intensity. I figure I'll walk until exhaustion, rest, then trek hard before the sun is directly above.

I lightened my load in the bathroom garbage of a Taco Bell. After a modest dinner yesterday, I reduced the 55-pound initial weight to 38. There's more room for improvement, but there's only so much loss I wish to bare at one time. I've already said goodbye to 100 bags of oolong tea, a liter bottle of water, two collared t-shirts, all my heavy jeans, and excess odds, ends, and trinkets. I'll strip it down further when I'm in more of a gung-ho mood. Soon, I'll have only what is necessary for survival. Publix has become for me what a truck stop weigh station is for a tractor-trailer.

I acquired two 24-ounce cans of Miller Lite in replace of food, today. It was a good move on my part. Around noon I was sipping on them while sitting on a bus stop bench, just absorbing the day from my vantage point. I took a Sharpie and tattooed my Big Green Monkey with all of the band names that have influenced me. I regard them as being part of what made me who I am. I did the same thing to my black military boots when I was aboard the

Coast Guard Cutter Alert. I used a White-Out pen that time. No one seemed to notice.

Day 3: Rain is a comical thing. Last night it began to pour down with the force of a man who had to wait in line for the toilet at a busy bar. I hesitated little before I opened my bag and retrieved my poncho. I had two of them, so I did my best to drape one over the monkey, too. What are friends for? If my belongings get saturated, this will be the beginning of a very miserable trip. And with moisture comes bacteria, mold, and the odor of gym socks I'd sooner try to avoid. As it stands, the friction created from normal walking movement has allowed the monkey to shave raw patches in the protruding portions of my back. It's sanding down my bones. Damn this wicked spine! Imagine what damage and discomfort would ensue if the monkey were suddenly heavier.

I happened by an overturned shopping cart by one of the less fortunate types of bus stops. They're the kind possessing no benches, but rather a simple post marking its place in an effort to get the metro drivers' attention. Someone, who had since moved on, was using this cart as a makeshift chair. I followed suit and "popped a squat" for a moment. There was a tree behind me with branches extending beyond myself just overhead. It was a natural dome to help ward off the full impact of the rain. The monkey shared this "seat" with me. I didn't want it sucking up rainwater directly from the ground.

Being a former plank rider, or maybe because I've watched a lot of movies, an idea came to me. I could give my back a break by pushing my Big Green Monkey in the shopping cart. It was late enough that I wouldn't see too many people. No one was traveling the road. I could feel less like a bagman, lady, whatever, without the eyes of judgment cast on me. What the hell? After the rain subsided a bit we were on our way. I stood on a crossbar and kicked with my right foot. I rode the cart like a racing skateboard, down the sidewalk for many blocks. My Big Green Monkey played the role of ET as we sped along into the night.

What does a 99-cent poncho look like, you ask? Picture a large, thin garbage bag with three holes and a hood. Mine was bright blue to make it more shameful and obvious.

This adventure reminded me of Lieutenant Dan—Gary Sinise, in *Forrest Gump*. He was in the crow's nest of the ship during a heavy storm, confronting God and the Heavens. Perseverance with a twist of comedy& insanity… What will the next day bring?

Day 4: The heat is so intense today that I ducked into Riviera Beach Public Library rather than melt like candle wax. That's right kids, I'm back where I started. The library is on the crossroad that connects Military Trail to US 1. If I kept walking passed the intersection for US 1, I'd eventually be on the beaches at Singer Island. I'm beyond the section where I was mugged and it only gets better the further north I travel from here. Earlier, I stopped by the Homeless Veterans Service office and donated the remainder of my excess clothing, including black ankle socks, more shirts, and even an ugly pair of shorts. I now have only four outfits with extra socks and Underoos. It felt good to give clothing to people who could distribute it to those in need. Who better than a veteran? My bag is lighter, but it's still no feather.

Day 5: Now I'm having fun! I walked through North Palm Beach last night, all the way to Jupiter—the city, not the planet. That would be ridiculous. I finally rested at Burt Reynolds' Park. I couldn't make this shit up. Surprisingly, the trees didn't have mustaches. I sat at a picnic table, in moderate shade, and finished *How to Get Ideas*, by Jack Foster. This was my second time reading it. I guess that means I didn't get the *idea* the first time. There are certain parts of that book I will discuss in a later entry.

I got the urge to move after a short nap on the bench part of the picnic table. I was giving my feet some air after popping nagging blisters on them with my pocketknife. There was probably more water in them than I had in my whole body last night. Fatigue was my antagonist, but somehow I made it. I took a few seats on damp grass, leaning my back against the Big Green Monkey. I was relieved from my workload and with that, I fell asleep for short naps each time. I used a drinking fountain at the park to regain what I had lost. Now I'm in the Tequesta PBC Public Library. The librarian had seen my CW 34 news piece. She wished me great success.

It's 91 degrees in the open sun. I can't believe I spent so much effort chasing the other rats. *This* is freedom. I have purpose and goals that are worth any amount of energy and sacrifice I make for them. This time, it's not all going into making someone else rich.

Day 6: I made it deep into Martin County, all the way to Jenson Beach. I'm sitting down at the Martin County Public Library, saturated in a unique sense of accomplishment. I had walked for many hours in complete desolation. Not only were there no monuments to consumerism, there were hardly anything at all. Trees and brush have been the only constants on this trip. I've been using roadside buildings I pass to fill up my water bottle. It's a very useful means to an end. There aren't many buildings that do not have outdoor faucets on one of their four sides. If it weren't commercial use property, that's where you'd also find the garden hose. Some establishments wrench off the spinning dial above the spout, or if it's a lever, close off the valve. Most do not think to, however, or can't due to some fire safety code I have only speculation of.

I learned that both in Stuart and Jenson Beach real down-to-earth people do exist. Through my interactions at convenience stores after that long stimulus-free stretch, it was uplifting to find people who still keep the forgotten practice of common courtesy alive. Here, it's as natural as dew on morning grass. Where I'm from it's so rare that when I do encounter it, I still find it novel. Back when I lived in West Palm the only thing that baffled me when meeting someone new was how, out of millions of sperm, *they* won the race. Was I looking at what became of the reluctant swimmer? Did they say, "What could possibly compare to what I just went through? Now if you need me, I'll be on the couch?"

The moment I got to a gas station I rushed in their bathroom for a shave, a scrub shower, and a quick wardrobe change. The Coast Guard "spit kit" is a handy shaving bag where I have all my necessities for a clean body stowed, including 3 sticks of antiperspirant. I don't even bother mentioning dental hygiene, because I brush at least three times a day as always. When dealing with a backpack that has everything stacked on top of itself it's very difficult to execute any of the mentioned functions. I end up having to take apart the bag and repack it every time. Then I have to be sure, once again, that nothing will feel bumpy, or be poking me in the back. The alternative would be to stay dirty, so I'm perfectly satisfied with the way I'm doing it.

Day 7: I got a chance on this misty day in Vero Beach to leave a message regarding my walk at the *Press Journal* newspaper's office. Around a bend of the road I ran into the McCain~Palin headquarters. There I took refuge under an awning while the rainfall intensified. I wrote a heartfelt letter of encouragement wishing them the best of luck. My naive hope was that some staff member would be moved by it, enough so to deliver it up the chain to the candidates themselves.

I spent the rest of the day reflecting and also planning as I walked progressively north. I have some serious finance issues facing me that are inspiring a negative train of thought. I don't even have a tent or a back-up pair of shoes. The tent shouldn't be necessary until I'm well on my way west. The shoes would be ideal, if only to allow mine to air out awhile and not get too rancid.

Day 8: I hate the French. This has no relevance to anything. I just like to say it every so often. It centers me.

Sunday, the day of new experiences, and some enlightening ones… I mentioned my financial woes, recently. I'm not lacking funds for the basic necessities, just yet. Even if I was, I'm resourceful, clever, and creative. My intention going into this was to do it as a survivalist. I had a good idea what it would be like. No one forced me to take this walk, therefore it is no one else's responsibility, nor are they obligated to feel any kind of emotion in any direction. I am not like the pieces of shit that beg me for change and pull scams. When I say I'm resourceful, take it for what it's worth. I am a student of the outdoors and I'm good at finding things I need. I'm not a hunter-gatherer by any means, but I do know how to make several types of snares. If there's some useful debris on the side of the road, I'll put it in my Big Green Monkey for future use. And most importantly, I've eaten rabbit and squirrel before and I'm not afraid to do it again.

What I am most concerned with is losing my website because the bill is due on the 22nd of October. Right now that's how I stay connected to the world. It's not a great expense. In fact it's very reasonable. I just need to find a way to make it happen by my deadline and all will be well.

I came to a Crossroads. No, really... That was the name of a Christian Fellowship I entered before making my way into Sebastian. I was hesitant at first. My soul has so many pockmarks on it that it looks like Edward James Olmos. If I were ever to sell it, it would have to be at reduced, scratch & dent pricing. I was relieved when I didn't burst into flames as I entered the double doors.

My head was a city of frantic thoughts. At any moment I could have lost control and freaked out over my website woes. I was mentally preparing myself to ask my parents for the thirty-five dollars. It would have to be at my next library stop. Time was wearing thin. With today being Sunday and tomorrow Columbus Day, there would be no library in the country open until Tuesday. Whiskey, Tango, Foxtrot! That is how us TCs, or radiomen, used to say, "What the fuck?" It was one of the more obvious in our collection. A man must maintain his image in the eye of sworn military code, after all.

Little things have been happening that prompted this visit to church. I have noticed very strong coincidences. Things I know would be useful, but were without, and the things I later discovered on the side of the road were too fitting. If not a perfect solution, it could be made to work. All I had to do is see a common item in a creative new way. It was as if someone had placed these items for me to pick up at just the right places and moments on the trail. It's a good thing I learned to look *down* whether hiking a trail or any path. It's a basic lesson included in most survival guides.

The same wisdom can be obtained from conversing with a drunken, homeless person. They scour the ground and asphalt for the little extras that make life more enjoyable. Things such as a half smoked cigarette, money for more hooch, and a partially eaten piece of chicken are priceless gems to these gentlemen of the streets. I think in my case, however, the events could best be summed up by the sayings, "The Lord will provide," and "He helps those who help themselves." It's just me and my monkey, but somehow I have the comfort of never feeling truly alone. I'm no mystic, but I'm not a man who seeks to debunk God, either.

I found the Crossroads Christian Fellowship just in time. My intentions were to attend services and leave. I wanted to be around people in a positive atmosphere. What I got was a whole lot more. I spent three and a half hours at the church in bible study. We ate chicken, had coffee and examined many sections of the Book. I noticed through discussion of passages, and songs sung, that the words, "path" and "walk" are repeated frequently both metaphorically, and in the literal sense. Was I being sent an unmistakable message? It's clear that I was intended to be there. I was being encouraged, and weight was being carried so I would not have to bare it all myself. I felt reassured that I had not gone mad, and my mission was again validated before my own eyes. I was receiving a personal message amidst the activity around me. That urge to call my parents and beg them for money turned into a desire to tell them I was doing fine. I wanted to tell them I love them.

I wish to thank the good people of Crossroads CF for awakening me to the underlying importance of my quest. It's easy to get locked in the *box* when all you see is what is visibly around you. I do not feel it was really their words, but rather a feeling, like another presence in the room. It was there, peeling back the layers, washing away the soot of negativity collected on me from living in the halfway house.

Day 9: Sebastian is my kind of town. The day has yet to begin, but I'm at a computer, catching up, transferring notes from the past three days of journal entries. I may as well say something while I have the opportunity. I'm at a Best Western, borrowing time in their business center. I locked my bag to a tree out by the road, and just wandered in as if I belonged here. I mainlined to the continental breakfast area where I ate four bagels, loaded with cream cheese and jelly. I also ate the traditional staples: eggs, sausage patties, and toast. After my 2nd foam cup of orange juice and 5th of coffee, I find myself in here, a small, tidy room. It's divided from the hall by a dark, stained wood door. It locks, too. I'm safer in here than I would be trying to take a dip in their pool or lounging in their welcome center. Sebastian is a beautiful, but very windy little town by the Indian River. Before I made it to the city limits, I passed by a roadside orange orchard. Being a Sunday in the South, they were closed. This was no grove stand. It had a full sized store adjacent to the fields of trees. I had to take cover under the roofed picnic area of the establishment. Rain had been skipping along behind me the whole day, paying little attention, and just taking its time catching up. Now it was here any very rambunctious. The timeframe for this was about an hour before I happened by the Crossroads CF mentioned.

After waiting out the irksome weather, I walked in still misty conditions heading north, of course. There were a few random, neglected trees, flush to the roadside, far from the rest of their best-in-show relatives. They were the outcasts, banished from their homeland for being an ugly embarrassment. They offended the more refined pillars of the orange tree community, and therefore were forced to live away from them in exile. They grew in grotesque patterns, reminding me of something I might find in a Tim Burton film. If not sex appeal, what they did have going for them were the ability to produce fruit. I've heard tales I only remember episodically, that Florida oranges can have a little green on the outside and still be delicious. I snatched two and continued on my way. I placed one in the right pocket of my cargo shorts and I began peeling the other. After the first taste of sweet decadence, I understood that the trees, like me, had a lot to offer. We shared a common bond. We were all misunderstood. From my experiences and interactions living in Dade City, Florida amidst the cows and orchards, I know I should have been fined $500 for each orange taken. That is the law created to protect the orange growers from theft. The Punk Rock Nomad Strikes Again…

"Got Crabs?" That should be the t-shirt sold to tourists that visit Sebastian, FL. As I was walking yesterday the sun came back out and was as intense as ever. Everything was damp giving way to favorable conditions for this brilliantly colored, but very suspicious type of crab. Its shell was an arrangement of violets, pinks, red and white. It got me thinking. In *Little Mermaid*, was not the crab named Sebastian? That little prick, the head with legs, could he have been a product of a creative mind who lived in or visited this area of Florida? I passed many of them on the road. They immediately got into a defensive posture, with claws raised to the heavens, as I approached. What I respected about them is their will to defend first and scurry away a distant second. That's evidence they have character. Way to be, crab.

I have roughly 19 miles to hump before I reach Melbourne. This is to be the site of my first major road change. I will head west on 192 until it's later renamed Irlo Bronson Highway, and further still to its very end. At that point I will walk 27 Northwest into the panhandle. I need to find a place to do laundry, today. I have a damp, musty towel, the one I use to scrub shower with, causing issues in my Big Green Monkey.

I've been sleeping on hard benches and it's beginning to take its toll on my back. Just this morning I awoke on one of these benches when a garbage truck was out doing its run. I was on the outskirts of a park, damned if I remember its name. This self-designated rest area was in front of a real estate business that provided my makeshift bed outside its doors. I chose this location because the wind coming off the river was too bitter to sustain in the openness of the park. Although light in nature, the precipitation was being whipped at me. At least here I had a building between it and myself. The rude, unordered wake-up call occurred at 5:30am. I, being a man of motivation, thought perhaps this was a good time to get going. Coming to terms with my exhaustion, I decided to lie back down. I was startled awake minutes later when a car crashed directly into the median, mangling and uprooted a street sign.

Tire screeching is loud enough to wake most people and the only noise I heard was as a result of the impact. I don't think these people ever slowed down. I saw a flat tire on the front passenger side. The car backed up from its plateau on the median, dragging the destroyed sign underneath. It managed, with the horrific sound of dragging metal, crunching fiberglass, and a grinding rim to take a left hand turn up a side road. I could see sparks coming from the now limp undercarriage as it did its best to speed off. They were definitely trying to avoid contact with police. If I *had* gotten up when I first thought to, chances are I would have been run down, just as the sign was, the moment I got to the road. Even if the car missed me by some slim margin—what then? If they were motivated enough to drive a wreck away, who's to say they wouldn't have been equally motivated not to leave any witnesses?

Day10: I don't know about baby, but Daniel definitely needs a new pair of shoes. Last night I walked 19 miles, give or take an inch, for a grand total of 25 for the day. In an effort to do so I got into a few stand-offs with crabs. I played soccer with one and taught it a harsh lesson in Darwinism. Forget, "Under my thumb" Mick Jagger. Try a round of *under my foot* after having kicked your ass for several feet. It appears these crabs aren't so gifted in the *art of war* after the sun goes down. If only I had my face paint…

I reached Melbourne a little after 1am. The wind was unforgiving, and blowing my Big Green Monkey and me off balance more and more as fatigue took over. I plopped my weary body down quite dramatically. There, in a tiny lawn behind a Christian Church I figured no one would dare fuck with me. I produced another layer of clothing from my bag and quickly put them on. It wasn't enough. Rain, wind, and little Danny, all alone with no shoulder to walk on, let alone cry… I dug into the Big Green Monkey once more. In a fit of exhausted rage, I finally extracted a promised solution to not-so-modern problems. On my knees in the damp grass, bag still open before me, I raised the treasure above my head and let out a victorious howl. I had my Coleman emergency blanket. It comes neatly folded in a 3" by 3" square. When at its maximum potential, it's large enough to cover a man only slightly taller than myself. It looks like tin foil with the texture and properties of a thin sheet of plastic. Being my first time using it, I figured I'd just wrap myself in it and set the oven to 350°. 30 minutes later potatoes are done! The material helps keep your body heat from escaping. The trade off is you look like an injured alien lying on the ground. A potential passerby may think the invasion has come. A couple of times the rain kicked into high gear, and woke me. For the most part I managed to ignore it. The blanket is plastic, therefore waterproof. I covered my head and went right back to sleep. Before I made way, I paused for a moment to acknowledge that I was still alive. Unlike a home, everyday out here that I wake up is a direct result of the effort I took to assure that outcome. A man could get used to this. I felt more spiritually connected to the Earth than I would have in favorable conditions.

If anyone has the impression that I'm vacationing in self-indulgent luxury, they're mistaken. I can't honestly tell you that some sick, adventurous part of me isn't loving every second of it, however. Both discomfort and pleasure are eagerly gobbled up by that part of my personality, but it doesn't speak for the rest of me. In fact, the rest of me doesn't associate with it. He's never invited to parties with the rest of me because he's not paper trained, and he's bound to seduce someone else's date.

I made it to 192 shortly upon awakening. Ah, my first major road change of the trip… I have only 65 miles before the next one, but it's straight through alligator territory. Much like my Best Western burn, I crept into a Days Inn to type out my notes, today. All they had for me was coffee and cereal, but I was strangely comfortable with it. Milk offends me, so I eat mine dry. Once my two dollars are gone, grocery stores and gas stations will become unofficial sponsors of the trip. Hey man, all is fair in love and suburban jungle survival.

Day 11: I walked in completely barren land for what seemed like an eternity. It was the type of walk you take if your goal is to have some sort of religious experience. Did I mention that the majority of this stretch is comprised of swamps known for their dense population of alligators? There's nothing but marshes and creeks to my right, all festered with mosquitoes and gnats. There's a thick, overbearing odor all around. Imagine, if you will, a mixture of manure with humid algae from stagnant waters. I'll have mine shaken, not stirred, please.

I had two separate people turn around after passing and offer me a ride. I graciously declined both offers. The plan was to walk, not take rides, even if I am 34 miles from any substantial sign of life. If this *was* a temptation of the devil, it was met with honor and devotion to my chosen duty. I was extremely fatigued, had run out of water, and knew I'd be making camp under the stars, that night. It would be a roadside table for one, with the possibility of meeting up with a party of reptiles later.

I will not deny myself one moment of this experience that's destined to change me and make me weirder. "Danger" is *my* middle finger. Shortly after stepping over a carcass of a young alligator, likely the victim of a hit-and-run, I sat down on a grassless patch of hardened sand. What a relief having the Monkey off my back. I sweat clear through the canvass material of it. I could see white salt lines on the outer edges of the wet area. Although the sun had long left this day, the moon was full, providing more than enough light to make out detail in things. Thanks for the nightlight, Lord. I definitely appreciate it, if only to see a predator before it sees me.

Earlier in my walk I happened to be looking down, as trained, and discovered craftwork. It was a crucifix made from a plastic knitting sheet, the ones that look like graph paper. Whoever made it used light colored yarn. I took the message at face value without question. I was being told that I'm not alone on this walk and to keep up the good work. It was heartwarming, or maybe I was having a heat flash. I picked up the craft and held it before me in my right hand as I carried my open pocketknife in the other. I felt like a crusader, except I wasn't out to kill anyone. I was on defense. If attacked, I'd make damn sure I was ready. The cross is still in my pocket, now. I'll be keeping it.

I'm going to try to sleep. I'm sure writing in the moonlight will degrade my vision eventually. Here, atop my poncho, I am in bed for the night. I'm no more than four feet from the road's shoulder. I hope no drunk drivers swerve toward me. My Big Green Monkey is standing guard. I doubt I need worry on his watch.

<u>Day 12</u>: This morning I woke up only to find myself fully intact. Nothing had devoured me in the night. I was wide-eyed more often than asleep, anyhow.

Today's walk was full of nothingness. I was thirsty, and famished. This gave way to a certain dizzied high that made it difficult to concentrate. I got moving around 5:30am after shaking off the dampness of morning dew. I made it to the section of 192 known as Irlo Bronson Highway near 5pm. I was officially in mouse territory. I'm, of course, referring to the one who wears yellow clown clogs. I should make it to my friend's house by daybreak. He lives off of 27, a planned route of the trip. I have no real place to sleep until I get there. That's enough motivation to keep moving.

Day 13: (Cooper Memorial Library, Lake County): I underestimated the distance I had to travel. I didn't arrive at Dustin's until 9am this morning. This is a rest stop. I have no other friends, nor acquaintances in the upcoming counties or states. I'm going to be here for the weekend refreshing, regrouping, taking advantage of a real shower, and waiting for my sponsor to send this ominous, still elusive, representative he keeps promising. I have a feeling I'm about to be greatly disappointed. This rep is supposed to be delivering me funds and supplies. The golden chariot has yet to cross my path, however and my suspicions have grown. This morning, sleeping on the loveseat seemed warm and inviting, but I just couldn't do it. I've been conditioned to hard surfaces, so I made my place on the floor with a throw pillow. I'll continue to keep those who might care informed of my daily goings-on throughout my stay in Clermont. Every moment of this experience is crucial to the accurate depiction and delivery of the story. I am your road scholar, and makeshift journalist on this bizarre ride. I assure you're in good hands. I have unwittingly become more of a reporter than a fiction writer, but I'm embracing it for all its worth. In addition, I've taken on the collateral duty of photographer, with 5 disposable cameras already filled. I don't particularly trust them to deliver decent, visible media, but it's all I have at the moment.

Clermont is a beautiful, little hill town. Your eyes aren't deceiving you, and you probably aren't suffering from organic brain dementia. There are hills in Florida! When I used to sell loans in this state the whole grid map was deemed a flood zone. Much like myself, Clermont bares the stigma of the rest of the lot.

I've been practicing basic skills for survival whenever I have a free moment, and when I'm out of view of any judgmental eye. Today, before arriving at the Library, I tested my fire-making prowess. Using a flint and my pocketknife, I managed to create a spark great enough to ignite a patch of cotton saturated in petroleum jelly. I threw a little kindling atop and provided air via lungpower until I had a decent flame. I took a lot of pride in this little event. I gained more self-assurance and felt less humbled by the challenges that may lie ahead. I'm learning a lot about myself, and strengths I never knew I possessed. After all, I was a willing participant in superficiality for many a moon. It leads me to believe that we all have it in us, if self-preservation is still an instinct we haven't lost.

I left the Big Green Monkey at Dustin's place. I feel incomplete, naked, without it. I should go do laundry. That way I'll have a reasonable excuse to reunite with my monkey and lug it around once again. Sitting here in this godforsaken library, my thoughts are with it. I wonder how it's doing. Jesus Jones, Tom Hanks! What's your problem? Every reference I dream up has to do with one of your perfectly executed performances. Shit, if that is my fate, I hope only that I don't have to jump into a volcano or discover that my neighbors are cooking bodies in their basement furnace.

Day 14: I'm killing time, awaiting word from my estranged sponsor. I'm about to leave Clermont with or without supplies. I made a commitment to myself to wrap this little dance up in 150 days. No suit is going to delay that due to their own lethargy. It will derail the psyche and motivation in place. Lying about like this could lead to doubt, complacency, and oblivion. I won't allow it. I am on a mission. As Thompson said, "This is the American Dream in action." I sense he was being facetious, but I am not.

At a bar I met a man named Troy. His girlfriend was serving me Seadog Blue Paw that I was able to purchase with motherly funding. After speaking with him, I learned his passionate hobby was survival camping. Fate? Alcohol? Both? Later he came back to the bar with a large, rolled sheet of Tyvex that I could fashion into a tent. All I needed was parachute cord to tie it off. What a great guy. He just saved me $35-60. Of course I immediately ordered another, with this newly released monetary burden. He taught me a lot of useful strategy I could apply if and when the situation called for it. Troy, Shauna, I am forever grateful.

Another barfly named Lizzie gave me a new gray bandana to help keep the sweat from irritating my eyes. People DO fucking care. Right there I was sure I was on the right track. America was in this bar. It was on the streets. It was no longer a concept, but a manifestation. It was the child being pushed on a swing by a single father. It was a random conversation in a bar. It was kindness, humanity, and love. That's why I say nothing flattering about the government and yet I'm passionate about America. WE are the heart. WE the People are what make this country great. It's time we showed our influence and strength a little more. If not follow me, then who? Follow yourself. Get off your ass and effect positive change. If you don't, silence your complaints for you have revoked your right to do so. Nearly fifteen days ago I caught a fever, a passion for my task-at-hand. Outdoor survival? That's just scraping by. I'm aimed at outdoor *thriving*. I need to get back on the road. I want to see what's around the next bend before I lose the importance and meaning behind these random, yet purposeful encounters.

Day 15: "Did you forget who you are?" -Perry Farrell, *Did You Forget*

If you haven't noticed, I'm going on blind faith that you, the reader, have a lot to offer. I believe in you and I've never met you. Don't judge me too quickly as being arrogant or cocky. I act that way as a tool to hold myself to a standard I, myself, wish to reach—a goal. First Man must envision his goal, live as if it's already been achieved, and think as a champion. The rest falls into place. That is the gist of the aforementioned writing of Jack Foster.

Presently, much to my chagrin, I am still without a few vital supplies. It appears that tomorrow I will be walking into the unknown with a lower chance of success unless I get creative. I have made it this far by anticipating and improvising. It's a more uncomfortable means to an end, but it works nonetheless. I have received a lot of moral support from locals and it fuels my fire more than they realize. Talk is cheap, so I understand it will take action to prove. I am grateful for both my new acquaintances and my old friends, Dustin and Alexandra. Tomorrow I'm back to playing solo on this little stage dubbed the "open road." I will continue my attempts to sustain life in the face of foreign obstacles and strange conditions.

Day 16: I'm at the library for the last time, but not to worry. Even if it should take me days before the next opportunity arises to updated the tracker, I'll have my journal on-hand. Pens don't crash, potentially losing all the valuable data recorded. They merely run out of ink, a problem easily remedied. And never once have I had to say, "My notebook is on the fritz."

I may have to begin hunting and picking berries & plants to eat. I'll only play a hunter's role if it is necessary for survival. I'll not march off and kill for the sake of feeling like a bad ass. There's no honor in that. Troy gave me a compact fishing kit that maybe I can put to use. It would have been helpful when I was still walking the coastline. If not in saltwater, there are countless networks of canals loaded with prey in shallow environments. Less habitat equals less food and a greater desire to eat whatever is dangled in front of them.

I'm taking to this lifestyle very well. It's the only possible way to achieve. If I was unmotivated, I would only impact my level of success in a negative fashion. Again, I'd be my own barrier between myself, and my proposed goals. I'm leaving that part of me behind. Hopefully I can bury it in a deep hole where it can no longer be a threat. If only this Big Green Monkey was feather-light, I'd feel like a warrior. This backpack is my constant reminder to stay humble, as it does quite literally, burden weight upon my shoulders. After a few *goodbyes* I'll be meeting up with 27 and taking it North. It's just under 22 miles to the next town of consequence.

Day 17: I made it to Leesburg sometime after 10pm. I crossed paths with a gentleman headed in the opposite direction, to Haines City. Charlie, the fellow traveler, was in Austin, Texas eleven days ago. Through hitchhiking and manpower, he was almost to his destination, already. He gave me cigarettes from his hiking pack, the kind with the metal frames and a spot reserved for sleeping bags. He was about my height, unshaven, and at least fifteen years my senior. He wished me luck after some brief chitchat, and I gave him the same respect.

After parting ways with him, I walked just a little further before I found my first real gem of the trip. There on the ground was a PBC pipe, about an inch thick and 5 feet long. I had myself a synthetic walking stick. The marvels of modern technology! Not too long after that I happened across a mint condition rollout mat. It was made from straw and sturdy, blue stitching. If the mood strikes me, I can now do Yoga exercises! Oh, and it will provide and alternative to sleeping directly on the ground. I pulled the cross out of my pocket and kissed the dingy little thing. Someone was leaving treasures out for me to pick up.

I still managed to make my bed on a pile of ants. Even with my alien costume wrapped around me, I awoke several times to very sharp pains. I moved a little further north and found a grassy spot out of the way of traffic, only to find that the ants had already established another camp there. This morning, with the gradual illumination marking the new day, I was able to see all the little white bumps on my arms and legs, evidence of their attacks.

I've since upgraded my PBC pipe to a real hardwood stick. It's taller and less flimsy. I figure I walked a total of 26 miles last night and into this afternoon. Whenever I found something clever I accessorized my latest walking companion. I crisscrossed flat rope to fashion a handle grip and shoulder strap. The bottom end splits off into a small "Y." I was able to rig the fishing line to it and a metal washer as a base, so I would not be able to stab it too deeply into soft ground and wreck my newly created pole.

Car 54, where are you? I gave up on contacting my sponsor. I left several messages and sent plenty of e-mails. It's better to adjust my plan excluding any assumed assistance now, before I get stuck in a desperate position later. I can't relax on something, thinking it's already been addressed and handled.

I'm sitting at a picnic table in Roger's Park resting my feet. I forgot to mention, that my motherly funds didn't just go to intoxication. The day before I left Dustin's, I walked eight miles roundtrip to Pay Less and picked up a pair of Champions. I figured the name suited the mindset, and they felt comfortable. I must have tied them too tight, or needed to break them in gradually, because the low cut top wore my right ankle raw. My sock was sticking to the fresh wound in a bloody mess. It had become part of the scab, so peeling it off wasn't any kind of fun. The cut was all filmy and slimy under the sock and it smelled like cheese. It couldn't possibly turn that fast, but the message was clear. I needed first aid to at least stop it from getting any worse, if not heal. I'm going to be walking and rubbing everyday. The wound will likely be with me the rest of the hike. Once injured in a spot like that, it's just a matter of dealing with it as a new companion.

My direct deposit for my last payroll check hit my account just before my arrival at Dustin's. With it I bought a $30 Net 10 phone with 300 minutes of airtime included, the ankle butchering shoes were divided between motherly funds and my own, some fire-starter sticks, another poncho, socks, an inexpensive hooded sweatshirt, some canned food, various cheap supplies from the Camping isle of Wal*Mart, and of course plenty of hop & barley pop. I can't seem to find a blowgun and it would be ideal for taking down a rabbit or squirrel. I picked up two more disposable cameras under $4 each, as well. It occurred to me I hadn't disclosed how I was able to fund the website for another three months. I spent $35 toward keeping it up and running. My mother, the saint she is, also helped me out, greatly. I have about enough change and singles to do laundry a few times and maybe eat off the cheap menu at fast-food locales for a week.

I'm sick of ants... Not sycophants. I slept on the bench of yet another picnic table here, today. It was semi-comfortable until I awoke, stiff of spine and contorted in pain. Even so, I walked the park's canal system eager to try out my new fishing device. I passed by a lot of curious birds, the likes of which I had never seen. There are numerous wonders in, and varieties of, Florida wildlife. Too bad all I could think about was bashing something over the head with my walking stick and seeing how they tasted. I saw a lot of fish, but none wanted the balled bread I had found. There was a decent sized alligator sunning itself on a piece of protruding industrial debris at one bend of the waterway. I pause and looked at it for a while. I was still thinking like a predator, "How could I kill this fucker and eat him?"

I hope tonight doesn't include a cast of ants playing the parts of the little men in Gulliver's Travels. I don't want to wake to find myself tied to the ground, helpless to whatever demise they choose. With every step feeling like gritty salt being rubbed into my wound, it's likely I will not make it too far. I will go light until have chance to heal.

Day 18: There are a lot of treasures to be found on the ground. There's an array of the useful, interesting and the odd. I'm looking for some items I can fasten the Tyvex with. From the mat I mentioned, to various scraps of rope, metallic items, etc., I'm beginning to worry that this is going to be too easy. I seek adventure, challenge, and excitement. I'm sure I'll find plenty more of that, too. I still have to conjure up food.

Today's creativity and improvisation didn't come from an inspirational piece of junk, however. It was in the art of finance. I had extracted my account funds days ago, but my bank, or the ATM I encountered, hadn't been privy to the information as of yet. I withdrew the funds a second time, intentionally putting myself in the red. I scored a much needed $140 through a technicality. Knowing I could not do it again, there was a period of buyer's remorse experienced, but I'm still relieved to have it. I'm doing an awful lot of sight seeing on this tiny budget.

The thing is, I no longer have sponsorship. Desperate times, insert cliché. I used my monetary advantage to get bandages, Neosporin, medical tape, iodine, and a small bottle of hydrogen peroxide for sterilizing cuts. I got a fistful of Tabasco Slim Jims, a stick of pepperoni, and a block of extra sharp cheddar, as well. I must be careful how much I acquire at one time, for it creates additional weight for me to tow.

With the sponsor out of frame, I now have more freedom to write this book and do this trip as it comes, rather than have to worry about public image or the confines of posterity. My made-for-TV, after school special just became a more honest depiction of firsthand events. No longer will I feel compelled to be unilaterally plot driven. I have a title for the book, but being that I'm afraid of theft, I'll keep it to myself for the time being. *Suspicion* is a sound system of checks and balances.

I miss Alice. The woman has my heart and I've carried her and the kids with me this whole time. She remains the best part of who I've been for the last two years. I know, even if no one else can understand it, that with every step I take farther from her, I'm getting closer to an inner peace. Once I can calm down, and say I made my best effort published author or not, I'll be able to give more of myself to our vision of a family and a future. This is my motivation. She is in strong opposition, and yet without her I feel I'd be a weaker man.

I'd be in rough shape if it weren't for fast food places and Wal*Marts being in such frequency along this trek. Public libraries allow me to update my website and inform loved ones that

I'm still alive and well. Parks often provide an inhabitable place to sleep or rest. Police have yet to harass me I think partly due to the Big Green Monkey being military issue, and because I've approached them before they had a chance to question me first.

I will be succeeding in this quest, this mission, using only *my* resources and planned strategies. This is the essence of what I've been searching for. It's a chance to see what I'm made of through challenges absent in modern living. I can only have an idea, but never know exactly what to expect with each step placed, each passing day.

Next Stop: OCALA. It's 29 miles northwest from where I am. My back is causing me a lot of trouble. It feels worse when I release the Big Green Monkey, than when I'm carrying him. It's painful enough to cry out.

Day 19: I made very little progress yesterday evening. I've only just entered Marion County. My right ankle is grated like cheese. It's oozing and hypersensitive. I'm in a little farm town known as Fruitland Park. With no real choice in the matter, I'm lounging out here today and giving my wounds a break. I found a cozy rest area known as Gardenia Park, and it's located flush to a library. When you're a man in need of a place to rest and a place to use a computer this is the type of scene you only dream of. This is the type of combination made only in Heaven. From interaction with the staff librarian, I learned there's a *Pubix* about three miles down the dusty side road I walked here on. Seeing that there were grills at the park, I decided I'd buy something to cook and have a nice picnic, if only for a morale booster. It gets lonely on these roads when all you have is a tightlipped Green Monkey to keep you company. Missing Alice and the kids, I figured I may as well saturate my brain with a fermented beverage and self-medicate.

I chained my constant companion to my chosen picnic table using the bike chain and my padlock. Then I ventured off into pastures and barren fields trusting that the information I received was accurate and true. There is some sort of road maintenance occurring on this rural route. The dust created a khaki colored fog as I pressed on. I stopped and talked to a local who was having a garage sale. He was a scruffy chap with beer-in-gut and a sparkle of intoxication in his eye. I made purposeful, polite small talk as I scanned for more supplies amidst his junk. I told him I'd be back through this way once I finished my store detail.

Having eaten much sand, and noticing a layer of dust particles on my clothing, I finally reached my destination. It was a plaza full of a variety of stores. It sure as hell felt like more than three miles' walk. Maybe it was the anticipation of grilling, because I love to cook. Most people who have a lot of passion make decent chefs. The only real exceptions to that rule are those whom have yet to discover the art, and embrace it. I bought what I think were called leg quarters. I'm used to buying boneless, skinless breasts, but I want to make my remaining money stretch. This huge pack of chicken was only $3.33, half of 666, but I'm Daniel. I should be able to live amongst the evil without worry. I fancy myself one of the chosen odd balls. I'm not quite saved yet, but I'm in no danger of becoming damned unless I, myself, consciously choose to be. The way I see it, I'd have to throw the game like the fabled White Sox, Shoeless Joe excluded, for that to be my fate. With the chicken, I also bought the cheapest package of hot dogs I could find at an overpriced *Pubix* location, generic hickory barbecue sauce, white bread, a small packet of herbs, and Red Hot sauce. I finished out my shopping with a trip down the cold beverage isle. There I found a 6pack of Natural Light and immediately perked up. I knew what was coming and I couldn't wait to escape the intensity of thought, if only for a little while. On my way back a speeding van screeched to a halt in front of me. As I approached it, grocery bags in hand I recognized the passenger. It was the gentleman who had hosted the garage sale. He asked me if I wanted a ride back, and I graciously accepted. The van was gutted out, full of garbage, scattered tools, and Busch Light cans. He had an open beer in his lap, as did the driver. Through conversation, I learned the proprietor of the vehicle was originally from Texas. They dropped me off in the library parking lot with an invitation to stop by if I wanted to get high later. I said I'd try in an effort to be polite, but that really has never been my cup of tea. It's never a good idea to make a hyper kid paranoid. There's no fun for anyone involved in that scene.

As I was gathering sticks from the ground to build my grilling fire, I noticed a pool toward the back of the little park. No one was in it. I found it rather odd because it had been unbearably hot since 9am this morning. Surely someone would have taken advantage of an opportunity to cool off. This would have been a perfect place to get clean, but it wasn't in the cards. Posted on the fence was a sign indicating the pool was closed for the season. The season? What season? This is Florida. Seasons are as follows: Hot, and hotter. The only real variance is felt in the evenings when the temperatures drop a little more than usual.

Some locals showed up at the park and took a seat at a table adjacent to mine. Two girls and one young guy were looking me over. They had a curious, but friendly aura about them. I spoke up, introduced myself, and offered them food if they were going to be around after it was cooked. I gave the young guy a beer and soon the four of us were sitting together. Later, after filling our guts with an impressive lunch, they left for a moment and returned with a loaf of bread, peanut butter, and a bunch of bananas as a gift. How did they know I was an Elvis fan? That was food fit for the King.

I had a very disappointing phone conversation with Alice. She reassured me that her views had not changed, and that I was an asshole. I think she just plain misunderstands me from top to bottom. Maybe she's waiting for me to say something that I cannot. I'm not going back home. Not yet. To do so would mean that I had given up on myself, my vision, and went back on my word.

I tried contacting my sponsor via e-mail and phone once again. It's obvious. I am on my own less the random acts of kindness from good-hearted Americans like these kids I encountered. I inspired them with my story and they, in turn, had inspired me. This is the type of interaction this mission is all about. I'm on a campaign trail. The difference is, I'm not looking for anything for myself, except good stories to share in my book. I know I'm on the right track in spite of the total lack of support I'm receiving from loved ones, and from professional reps that seem to have dematerialized.

Bellevue is 10 miles Northwest. Beyond that, Ocala. I'll have to take ALT 27 at some point through unfriendly neighborhoods as I make my way to Tallahassee. If I were intelligent, I'd let the wounds heal longer. I cleaned them up as best as I could expect to. I've air-dried most of the skin that once contained blisters full of fluid, applied antiseptic where necessary, and spackled everything with the Neosporin. I have a sense of urgency and a stubbornness that won't let me relax. Once I make a plan, I don't have an easy time focusing on anything but.

Day 20: Did I mention how much I dislike ants? I'm sitting by a computer in a Holiday Inn Express. I'm not here to stay, only to update. I did the math. Since I left, I have averaged 23.75 miles of progressive walking each day. I took 2.5 days off in Clermont, my one and only pit stop. 19 days minus 3 is 16. 380 miles divided by 16 is 23.75. I predicted I would accomplish 24 miles per day at 3mph. My calculation was almost exact. Even with an ailing back, uncomfortable footwear, an open cut, and countless blisters, I've kept a steady go of things. I only advanced about 14.5 miles, today. It's late night, and locals had warned of a dangerous ghetto ahead best reserved for daytime hiking. I'm traveling ALT 27 to the merger routes19/98/27. If I can't get away with an I-10 commute, I'll take 90W once I reach Tallahassee. Both roads will get me across the state line and into banjo playing, Alabama territory.

I visited a place called Intensive Care Ministries. There I met Anthony, Sheena, Krista, and Roger. They helped by allowing me to get my wounds and body clean at their facility. I owe them a lot. They took photos and treated me like a celebrity. I mention their names to remind myself who to give back to when I'm in a position to do so.

No rain, no pain. It poured all night in Bellevue so I took refuge and slept beneath the overhang of a closed business. I shivered convulsively under my thermal alien costume. The cold concrete was sure to wreak hell on my back in the morning. I have spinal arthritis. Cold equals Bad. The weather didn't improve much by morning. Fearing the owners would be opening up shop soon, I trekked out in the mess anyway. After a short, disgruntled phase my mood improved. In the elements, I felt more alive than I had in cozier confines of convenient life. Wow, say that five times fast... There's a feeling of comfort one can obtain in the strangest of places. I hadn't felt like this since I was a carefree child. I'm moving along with self-preservation in the forefront of my mind. That's all I need to focus on. Let's face it, walking isn't really a mind-consuming task. No matter how rough or uncomfortable it has gotten, it's always been equally as invigorating. I feel bad for the people locked in their cars passing by me. They are the unwitting prisoners of their own creation, and social design. I on the other hand, roam free and need very little. As they throw judgmental glances my direction, and in some cases shout something retarded, they are the ones in need of adjustment. They don't even know it.

My ankle wound smells putrid, this evening. I hope I don't lose it. I don't possess the dexterity to hop on one foot to California. C'est la vie.

Days 21-24: I am still alive, but there have been a number of close calls. Most involved wildlife and weather conditions as is to be expected given the nature of the mission. Ocala is the horse capital of the world, according to the sign. This town needs a glue factory! I have no interest in horses. The extent of my curiosity deals with how they may taste. I take issue with the concept of a pet costing more to board and feed than myself. I don't see the economics in that.

I walked for what seemed like months, passing hundreds of dangerous, poisonous spiders. Banana spiders are not indigenous to Florida. They were introduced through South American produce shipping. They aren't likely to kill you, but they can easily put you in the hospital for weeks. Huge welts, a feeling of semi-paralysis, and extreme pain are just a few of the things to look forward to if you accidentally wander into one of their vast webs. I had difficulty finding safe areas to rest. They were all over the tree line that was uncomfortably close to the road. Aside from the spiders and horses, there are huge estates all along this road. These places are more than just mansions. They are the castles of our country.

During the day I find myself hesitate to put on the poncho. It's a self-consciousness issue. I look crazy enough with the Big Green Monkey, and the walking stick. If I wear a garbage bag around I'll be dying of embarrassment. I know I'm not completely homeless, that I *am* going in a progressive direction toward a goal, but no one driving by me has the time to understand that.

Traditional conditioning has programmed my mind for what is unacceptable. "We mock what we don't understand." Dan Aykroyd said that in *Ghostbusters*. I find myself handing out my business card and over-explaining my appearance to people in effort to reroute whatever prejudice was forming in their heads. This walk is teaching me to let up on that anxious emotion, but it is not an instant change.

Williston was a death march. If I were Native, it would have been my Trail of Tears. I walked for 26 miserable miles before reaching "downtown." There I setup camp, i.e. my mat and torn thermal blanket. I was outside in absolute nothingness. I awoke to the sounds of crying babies—coyote. Mixed in with that was a sound much closer. From my experiences living in Dade City, FL I knew this to be the unmistakable warning signal that boar were nearby. Angry pigs with impaling devices as teeth, the kind that think nothing of tearing one another apart, would have no problem mustering up the courage to ruin *my* evening. I gathered my things with lightning speed and took to walking along the road once more. I have been hearing coyotes often, but the pigs were a new addition. I don't think any amount of charm or rational plea works with their kind. I carried my knife in hand. I would be no match for them, but I could at least scar one up before I succumbed to my own wounds. There was a light up ahead, an entrance to a planned development. I made camp there the rest of the night against a decorative brick wall. Bitter wind was cutting into my soul. I added another shirt layer, but that was all I could do. I was exhausted. My spine was a foreign object my body was rejecting. I did my best to sleep in the woodchip scattered grounds. Three more hours and the sun would be in the sky.

With sticky, bloody ankles, knotted shoulders, and a back that screamed to be put out of its misery, I made it to a gas station. It was just before 9am. I did very little walking the rest of the day. At night I built a fire in a cigarette bucket outside a bank. I let the fire burn down to hot coals and then slid it under their outdoor bench to act as a makeshift heater. It worked beautifully. I still only got a few disjointed hours of sleep due to all my aches and pains, but it was the best rest I had since leaving Dustin's house.

I trekked out to Bronson in the morning. It was a simple 13-mile burn through more nothingness. When I arrived in town I voted at the courthouse. What kind of example would I be setting if I didn't exercise my Constitutional rights?

The world is a big place. This becomes more apparent when you're walking the whole damned thing. Locals in Bronson told me I only had another 13 miles before entering Chiefland. I decided I'd go the distance. I speed walked with ferocious energy and determination for three solid hours stopping only briefly to relieve the weight of the Monkey from time to time. It's what I do when I reach guardrails. I can sit on the support posts and not have to take the bag completely off, creating less work for me than if I had to lift it off the ground much in the same fashion I used the bus stops earlier on the trip. There was still no Chiefland, not even after the 4th hour. I felt betrayed. I was very audible about it. There wasn't anyone around to hear me complain, anyway. Darkness consumed my backdrop soon after 7pm. The temperature fell dramatically, and icy wind ripped through the trees. I could hear canine in the distance. They sounded like domestic dogs rather than coyote, but how? There weren't any homes around and the noises came from everywhere. They were likely wild, and probably hungry.

I finally made it to an abandoned building where I took refuge against the wall that blocked the most wind. There I found damp wood and twigs to start a fire. I used the cotton balls dipped in petroleum jelly and a flint rod to get things started. Soon I had to douse the fucker with lighter fluid so the moisture could burn out of the wood. It was a more needy fire than my previous one. I spent most of my time trying to keep it going in the hopes I could finally rest beside it. I spread the coals out in a straight line across the ground. I made the line match the length of my body and snuggled up to it as close as I could. It was so cold I wanted to just lay right on top of it. My key chain/compass also has a built-in mercury thermometer. It read 40 degrees. My thermal blanket was shredded and useless. I improvised with the poncho, and covered my legs, which were bare below the knees. I prayed a little.

The next morning gave rise only to illumination, not temperature. It was rough weather, and I had no choice but to get motivated. My back protested every little movement I made. I was very hungry, partially dehydrated, and unbelievably exhausted.

I've been consumed with thoughts of my loved ones. I miss everyone terribly. I want to see the kids and take them to the park by our house. I have so many fond memories spending time with them. I want to cook a complicated and delicious dinner for Alice. I want to hug my parents, my brother, my sister, hell even my uncle, and tell them I love them. It will have to wait.

This is my chosen mission. The stranger and more difficult it gets, the more my challenges will sculpt me making me stronger. I hope to retain whatever wisdom I acquire for the rest of my days. It's come to the point now where I desperately need a hotel stay. I can no longer ignore my ankle woes. I must tend to my wounds and temper my passion to just keep marching into the sunset. Deadlines are out the door. I made them when I had no concept of my undertaking. I'd rather experience more and write a better story. I'm here to experience, so why rush through it? Well, because more time means more necessities like food. My funds are diminishing, not building. I need to reassess the details of my overall plan. Adjustments must be made. The deal was, I'd do this a certain way provided other things were in place. Without sponsor support, it's a whole different animal. One thing I've learned out here is that a person mustn't be too rigid. Things will be thrown at you, you will not have anticipated. Flexibility is necessary to adapt to an ever-changing collection of obstacles. Do so, or Darwin will getcha! If this *is* a survival hike then I will do what it takes to survive. I'm glad I set out with a premise, a set of principles, and a structured approach. If I can experience even more by doing something not originally planned, then why not let fate take me where I'm supposed to go? I am impulsive enough to trust the flow of things, so I'll not place barriers on something that sounds exciting, just because I'm afraid of breaking some rule. It's obvious by now that America did not respond. It's going to take the book to get their attention, not the event itself. In the meantime, I have to stay alive.

If I knew everything that was going to happen, or how it should go, then I wouldn't have had to do it. Peaceful Warrior said, "It's not the destination, but the journey that is important." I'm sure I misquoted it, but that's for my editor to discover. I almost missed out on my own message! Silly mammal! Unless bleeding or freezing to death, I will not flag down a vehicle. However, if I meet someone who strikes me as an interesting person, why not hop in if they take the initiative to offer me a ride? It could be a sign that my path is meant to alter in order to be enhanced. Aren't interaction, the human experience, and the random, bizarre shit that happens in between what makes a trip like this worth taking? I'm not just talking about rides, but I too may wander around and explore places not originally planned. I've learned I'm much tougher than I ever thought, having survived this long. The desert snake country of NM, AZ, and the Mojave will be a real challenge. One bite and goodnight. I still have plenty of time to worry about that.

Days 25-27: Happy Halloween from the road. I think I'll go as a slightly dusty, nomad with a larger-than-life backpack attached to him… What do you know? I'm already in costume! Since I've declared my freedom on this trip, and have license to follow my instinct, I have found the days to be abundant with possibilities. I happened by a gentleman pumping gas at a Texaco on the other side of Chiefland. He asked me if I needed a ride somewhere. "So soon," I thought. At the time I was consumed with details regarding survival in ever dropping evening temperatures.

      I asked him how far he was going and he said, "New Orleans, tonight. Then Houston." I struggled with the idea of taking a ride with Bobby, the person offering. He could see it on my face. I told him I was on a cross-country walk, but that I was injured and could use some time off my feet. I need to be able to exceed a snails pace, and by this time I had developed a limp. I took this as a sign. What are the odds some random stranger would be going that far in my direction? This road wasn't the quickest route to anywhere of value. He should have been at a gas station off of I-10, and not wandering around 27 this deep into a nameless town. Just when I couldn't get my head around the concept of walking any further, a solution materialized out of obscurity. Of course I'd take the ride. It's the only thing that seemed to make sense. Part of me felt I was betraying some part of my plan. Sensibility is still sensibility, however. In the end I let its influence guide my decision.

I've become very spiritual lately. From finding random items I needed, to the crucifix, and now this… Things have been seemingly working themselves out. I only have God and myself to talk to out here. What better road companion could I ask for? Now he's flashing a neon sign, guiding me to take this ride. If I deny myself, ignoring the voice that I've been relying on thus far, then I really would be off course. There was a reason for this occurrence. Adventure was awaiting me.

I threw my beloved monkey and walking stick in the back of his car-topped, Ford truck. Once seated I glanced down and noticed the blood had been flowing freely from my ankle. This opportunity for rest came just in time.

New Orleans: *This is not a town I could get used to.* We arrived at the St. Louis Hotel very late. Eagerly I rushed the unpacking process, gathered my hygiene bag and got into a hot shower. The heavens rained down on me. In there I became a new man. There might be something to that whole Baptism thing, after all. I scrubbed my feet and watched the water turn to mud as it rolled off my body. Half of my "tan" went down the drain. I wasn't smelly, but when you scrub-shower in gas station bathrooms for almost a month you sacrifice cleaning your feet so as to avoid catching some disease off the tiled floors. No, the shoes stayed on when I was in those places. What good are clean feet if they fall off? I'm not big on parasites, either. No one rides for free. I've never been a generous host in that sense.

Bobby Glass and I grabbed some beer from around the corner. It must have had gold chips in the bottle paint judging by the price. I was happy to let him pick up the tab. We went back to room 208 where I learned some disturbing things about animal social structure in the African Jungles, thanks to the Discovery Channel. Apparently Bobby didn't drink. What the fuck? I hate that. It makes me feel self-conscious when I'm trying to unwind. We both had had long days. I'm sure his concept of a long day didn't include wet, cold concrete, a fire that refused to cooperate, a plastic bag as a blanket, ANTS, and a seemingly endless death march. It could have. I'm not familiar with his hobbies.

The next day we sat at a café, in the patio section and ate French doughnuts. It was supposed to be some great, unique experience. It tasted like it's Italian cousin, fried dough and confectioners sugar. You don't need to spend what these people were to get the same effect. Bobby Glass read his paper and I did what I normally do. I'm a people watcher. I like to study their interaction and movements. I try to decipher how much of what they do is honest expression and how much is bullshit posturing, and insecure, self- conscious gesturing.

After doing a little asking around, I found a place on Decatur called Checkpoint Charlie's. It was a bar with a jukebox, pool tables, and a section in the back to do laundry. I found that to be an intriguing combination. What better than a Laundromat that provides an activity while you wait for your clothes to finish? Or, if perceived from the other end, a bar that has a facility providing some service that is actually useful... Ingenious. "Sorry hon, gotta do laundry."

"Again? You do laundry every Friday and Saturday night!"

There's nothing reputable about Bourbon Street. It's lined with live sex act venues, gay bars, and shitty dives. I don't see the appeal, I guess maybe because I still have a soul. No, it's Decatur for me. There you will find a variety of interesting little holes in the wall each with a different genre of music emanating from their open doors. Walking down this street is like changing channels on a radio.

Aside from eating a few bites here and there, I pretty much just relaxed. Bobby Glass is 50. He's not urging me to run about the town with him. I had no personal desire to witness the nightlife. It was time to recoup. Besides, the way I see it, I found my girl. If her and I can't work things out, then I'm going to just take up a consuming hobby and put my head down for the rest of my life.

We left the next day at 10am. Destination: Houston. There was a scene at checkout regarding the bill, but I was too locked in my own world to pay too close attention. I just nodded and agreed with Bobby. Granted, the nighttime desk clerk was snotty to Bobby when he checked in and said she didn't have to accept the price he booked his room for online. I think he was just making sure everyone in the establishment knew he was upset. He bickers like an old woman.

After a very amusing ride, one for which I drove most of as Bobby slept, we arrived in Houston. Mr. Glass owns an import-export company. It's small, not too many employees, but he does very well according to him. With all the photographs he showed me of his travels around the globe, I'm sure there's truth in his claims. We drove to the airport where Bobby was taking an eight-day trip through different parts of Mexico. He'd be in Mexico City just in time for the Day of the Dead. There, he was to purchase inexpensive apparel for resale in the states. He promised to catch up with me wherever I was and take me as far as El Paso, TX. There I could sell some of his products at a flea market setting. I was given an opportunity to earn much-needed funds before venturing off into the desert. The plan was to be his employee for a few weeks. This would give me a chance to send money to Alice, too. I was sold on the prospect.

I allowed myself to take a ride and by doing so I advanced a considerable distance, and may soon be gainfully employed. I also got to see New Orleans, somewhere I would not have crossed on the route I plotted.

We're just two newly acquainted friends, tearing a path due west in a pick-up truck, following whichever path seems most ridiculous, and discovering adventure along the way. Living has never felt more alive. Who knows what tomorrow will bring?

I learned one thing. After I get out of the Houston Library, I need to find the quickest path out of this fucking city. It's tall, pretty, and emotionally dead. I'm more at home without the suits and business monkeys giving me condescending glares rather than an answer when I ask for directions. Don't you get it? I'm trying to get away from you bastards. It's a win-win, now tell me how to do it quickly! McDonald's was the kickoff to my day. It was embedded in some high rise like so many Starbuck's before it. After assuring I had a gut full of violent grease, I happened into the library, three blocks away, and became a member.

I'm fairly convinced Alice has probably thrown away what's left of my belongings. This would include the only remaining hardcopy of my screenplay, a photo album I've put together through the course of my life, everything I wrote in high school and college, as if to erase my existence… She's hurt. I'm the "bad guy."

<u>Day 28</u>: "By the time the light has reached your eyes, the world has lived and died…"

-Peeping Tom, Neighborhood Spaceman

Not all Wal*Marts are created equally. The smaller, Dirt Marts typically have higher prices, and no alcoholic beverages. The stock items are of a limited variety, too. Their aisles are as narrow as European roadways. They are in a constant state of disarray, making their Feng Shui all *funked* up. This is Wal*Mart without balls.

Enter the "super center." In a *Great Wal of Mart* location, one can find a semi-respectable beverage selection, minus hard liquor. The overall product availability is much more expansive and vast compared to their black sheep cousins. Not all super centers carry the exact same items. One may showcase Chicago Cutlery knives while another may only have Faberware brand. The prices are so low that shoppers find themselves looking over their shoulder as they place an item in their cart.

Little differences in merchandise availability give each Great Wal of Mart their own signature and unique character. Every store has its own personality. The Great Wal of Mart gets to know each and everyone of its customers. It's consciously aware of their inner most retail thoughts and desires. It senses yearning and responds by assuring particular products are available upon, or shortly after a patron's arrival. With prices as they are, resistance is futile. It is able to eliminate the element of *buyer's remorse*. The Great Wal soothes the savage shopper, massages their metaphoric shoulders, and relaxes all resistance to purchasing.

<u>I'm about as Latin as a baked potato</u>: After sending e-mails and updating the web tracker, I walked out of Houston using Highway 290W's parallel service road. The nicest part of that city was the library. There are two in close proximity. One, a beautiful, old churchlike structure, and the other is a modern construction. I visited both, but the older one was reserved for city research, document achieving, and things of a more bureaucratic and lawful nature. Hence, there was no MySpace.com to be had.

I went in circles twice before I finally got to 290W. It wasn't a difficult concept. I was frazzled, and I made it more troublesome than necessary by misreading a few key signs. In this part of Texas 290W runs pretty close to the same path as I-10. It goes west, toward Austin, TX. I figured, "Why not take the one I know is OK to walk on?" Every major road has a secondary or service road where all the commerce is. That would be the best place for me. I had left the walking stick I've named "Mitch" in the back of Bobby Glass's truck at the airport. Mr. Glass had given me a little cash, money I did not ask for, to get whatever I needed until we met up again. My first thought went to *beer*, but I exercised some self-discipline. Food and a new map were top priorities. My compass was getting stuck in one position a lot, so I wanted to buy another one. I needed new socks, too. Then maybe, just maybe, I'd get the taboo product of my desire.

Right now, I just need to change my socks. Genius packer that I am, I put my weatherproofed bag of clothes in the base of my Big Green Monkey. It will be no small task retrieving fresh garments for tomorrow. I'll have to wade through, and shovel out three feet of miscellaneous, but valuable items before touching a stitch of fabric. I'm hesitant to fuck with the order of things because at present, there's a nice, flat cushioned area where my back touches. There's nothing more maddening than unbalanced weight distribution, or the aforementioned shifting object constantly jabbing me in the spine with each laborious step I take. Keeping myself injury-free is priority one. I have to be extra careful due to the spina bifida. Regardless, I'm going to make substantial progress. November 8th is a long ways away. I'd like to at least be in the next, major field marker of a town by then. Austin should be an achievable goal.

It's 10:17pm on this Halloween evening, 2008. As I sit on the outdoor bench in front of a Great Wal of Mart location, my bag securely locked beside me, I can't help but wonder how Alice and the kids are. I love my angel for better or worse, no matter what. Unless that *what* involved her getting involved with another. I don't think I should be around someone if she decided to process more sausage than Jimmy Dean. Not if I didn't want to end up in jail with blood on my hands, that is. It would have been nice to take the kids Trick-or-Treating...

I'm thinking about things I have no business being concerned with. I'm wondering if Bobby is really going to meet back up with me, and whether or not the prospective job offer holds any water. This is how it happens to people. Things you never planned on, never needed, make you dependent on them if you choose to alter the original course of action. I shouldn't even be curious about it. If it's meant to play that way, then it will. Obsessing over one possibility blinds us from seeing other opportunities when they arise. It could be a new idea all together that I'd miss if I'm too busy trying to force a different thought. Planning is poison to an open mind. I need to remember that. Otherwise I will fall victim to dependency on others, and that is never good. I like it when I have the freedom to suspect. Retention of control and power regarding one's own destiny is crucial to success. It is at the core of adaptive character values.

Yesterday I visited a Taco Cabana for the first time. It's a chain restaurant, but they make the best taco I ever had the pleasure of tasting. Mind you, I have been to Mexico's Baja peninsula several times. When I make a statement like this, it carries some weight of credibility. From the quality of meats and seasoning, to the fresh salsa island at the customer's disposal, the total dining experience is one of the best I've had even in my richest of days. Everything tastes authentic, rather than mass produced.

There were only two elements missing that could further enhance their establishment. I ordered a black bean burrito and found the beans to be slightly undercooked. I like them to be a little mushy. These beans possessed an almost crispy, structurally solid integrity undesirable for a burrito. The texture degraded the taste. Also, the salsa bar would benefit from the addition of an actual hot sauce. It would compliment their overall landscape, giving the final brushstroke to their masterpiece.

I suggest trying them out if ever given the opportunity. I've happened by two locations thus far, both located close to the road with Wal*Mart super centers nearby, recessed to the back of the parking area.

~A man stepping off his donkey couldn't remember what brand of jeans he was wearing, so he looked at his Ass.

~The bus read, "Not in Service." I've always wanted to go there.

Days 29-31: They say everything is bigger in Texas. As I was taking a piss in the cold, morning air I busted that myth. I'm getting a little frustrated with the sleeping conditions I've endured. I'm sure they're helping to build character, but less aggravation on my back would be delightful. Last night I slept in the fire ant infested territory near an irrigation canal. The canal held its form with a concrete mold. I rested on the upper edge of it without using my mat. I had on enough layers of clothing to cushion myself a bit, but at 56 degrees it was still a frigid experience.

I'm not getting discouraged with the trip as much as I am with myself. I wanted to travel a lot farther today. I came across a Gander Mountain location and couldn't resist wasting valuable time browsing all the guns and camping supplies I knew I could not afford. I used to get the Gander Mountain catalog mailed to me growing up in New York's cow and farm district. This was the first time I had ever been to one. I didn't even know it was a storefront. I figured it was a shipping warehouse, only.

Tonight's trip to a Great Wal of Mart will be for the soul purpose of shelter. If it weren't for there locations being so frequent, I don't know what I would do. I look up, legs tired, back aching, bag straps digging into my shoulders, and I see it. It's the sign glowing blue and white in the distance. The warm feeling of the Divine Hand comforts my weary body for I know everything is going to be all right. Since I didn't end up in a favorable area for camping, I'm going to have to improvise. I did that last night at the previous super center. After a certain time Wal*Mart will close off one of there entrances, locking it until morning. This means no traffic and lesser eyes. The only thing left to contend with is the slow moving, security patrol vehicle creeping up and down the lanes of the parking lot. His stealth is no match for my cunning, however. In the little tunnel meant to hold shopping carts, I fashioned myself a fortress and a bed. Using what I had, which were four of the multi-child carts, the kind with opaque, plastic molding, I set two of them on either side of a strip of three adjacent, regular carts. The child carts provided privacy while the regular ones, with their bulk-item bottom racks, made a short, jointed platform for me to lie on. I felt like fucking Einstein. That is, if he were a street dweller and had absolutely no desire to do math. I had little more room than a coffin, nestled between the metallic structures. Had I been larger I would not have succeeded in wedging myself in. Thank God for all those weeks of excessive poverty!

Listening to rats fight amongst each other, I did my best to sleep. It was difficult with my mind transfixed on the notion that diseased droppings were likely all around me. Would the dawn ever arrive?

I awoke cramped, sore, and in complete misery. When it gets too cold I have muscle spasms and cramps in my back and legs. I'm sure a certain level of fluid shortage is responsible as well. My calf was knotted. I had to pull on the bridge of my toes to stretch out the muscle. Then, the opposing muscles on my shin began to violently retract. I was fucked in either direction. I could see the muscles, deformed looking, in a higher position than normal. I have more *woes* than Joey Lawrence.

This is just daily life on the road, and a part of my life all the time. I normally omit descriptive details like this in an effort to sound less redundant, and so as not to whine or complain. I add it now, only to paint more of a picture of what I'm faced with in taking on such an endeavor.

This evening as I laboriously dragged my sagging ass into a Burger King, I took the Monkey right inside with me. I wanted to look over my notes and perhaps write a little more. The manager asked me if I had a website and immediately I produced a weathered business card from my front pocket. She said, "Yeah! I saw it. I've been reading the… What's it called?"

"Web-Tracker page. Get the heck out of here. How did you know about it?" I perked up, instantly.

She said, with wide admiring eyes, "A friend of mine. She is always on the computer. She was doing a search for something and your website came up. She clicked it and read the whole thing."

"How did you recognize me? The pictures are old and I've lost a lot of weight." I got suspicious.

"It's the bag. You describe it and there's that one page where you have a picture of the same kind."

I was convinced. This wasn't a put-on. She asked me what I wanted and gave it to me for free. I got the Fully Loaded Steakhouse Burger value meal. I overly thanked her, sat down with my food and busted out my notebook. It took me a minute before it occurred to me. My Big Green Monkey was more famous than I was. It's been stealing my thunder. I began writing furiously. Whenever I looked up I could see she had been looking at me. When our eyes met, she'd look away. I was grateful for being recognized, but only one girl will ever have my heart or my body... Even if she doesn't think she wants either right now. It wasn't always like that. There was a time, not too long ago, when I would have exploited this opportunity. When I was single, I was quite active. If these balls could talk...

A wise man once said, "Why loiter outside when you can loiter inside?" I think it was Jesus. There's a guy who did a whole shit load of walking. I bet his abs were magnificent! Having lingered about in front of this night's Wal*Mart for about an hour, I decided I'd look around inside. Most Great Wals are similar in layout, with exceptions going only to locations that were converted from a different business. In the far back of the store there's the employment center consisting of a computer and a chair. There are three bathrooms, the first two types being obvious. The third is a family restroom that you can lock for privacy. In the left-hand corner, swing double doors marking the entrance to the back stock, and employee area.

I washed up best I could in the family restroom. As I was walking out I noticed benches, like the kind I was occupying out front, along two of the walls. Why be cold if I didn't have to be? I felt like Goldie Locks, if Goldie Locks had a penis and drank malt liquor, deciding which of the three chairs best defined me as a person. I finally chose the one in the corner with most wall coverage to keep me out of direct view of the occasional passerby. I didn't have my Monkey. He was smoking a cigarette outside, secured to the bike rack. We've been hanging out a lot lately, and we both needed some alone time.

I was a little leery about spending too much of it in this location, with the "Associates Only" sign staring me in the face. There was steady traffic in and out of those backdoors. After all, that was the blue-shirts' cave. Deep within this store is a hidden world much in the fashion of Santa's workshop. Here, these diligent gnomes are hard at work assuring efficiency and maintaining organization. There is no crime in their tidy, khaki panted society. They were the first to fully adopt the concept of Utopian life. If anyone has ever watched Fragel Rock and has seen the little, green construction workers always building, and tending only to their business-at-hand, the picture becomes all too clear. Even with all this madness around me, I managed to fall asleep and not be bothered.

My version of the three-prong approach is relative to the conditions. I stopped at one gas station where I was able to scrub-shower using their bathroom sink and paper towels. Being concerned that I was already there for too long, I held off on shaving until I reached a convenience store. I try to move quickly and draw as little attention as possible to myself in all situations. I make efforts to be the guy you never even see, and never would suspect. I had to wrap up my shaving when rude, impatient knocking disrupted my daydream. I was finally able to brush my teeth at a third location. If anyone thinks I live the life of convenience, walk a total of five miles just to shit, shower, and shave some morning.

Reflections: (Revisited) Somewhere along 290W

I don't even think I knew up until now what has been driving me to press forward each day, and why this message is so important for me to get out to as many Americans as possible. There was a reason, deeply buried in an effort to take away the sting of its memory. It is what has driven me to become as spiritual as I feel I'm becoming, and as patriotic. I understand, as I walk through this hellish devil grass along 290W that I will make whatever sacrifices necessary to accomplish my mission. The dream is alive in all of us, even those who have unwittingly covered theirs in an *avalanche of ignorance*.

I'm dedicating this book and this trip to all of the Americans whose lives were cut short on September 11th, 2001. This walk is for them and their surviving families who have had to cope with such a loss. I'm not jumping on some popular marketing bandwagon. This is more heartfelt than I can bear. I am moved by the concept that men and women, facing eminent death on United 93, banded together and preserved the strength of their country at a price of their own lives.

NOTHING that I ever endure on this walk or in life will be enough to parallel the sacrifices made that horrific day in our Nation's history. I can only hope to appreciate and honor their efforts by doing something positive with the freedom they died to protect. If my part in the story is to remind people what a powerful force we are as Americans, then I accept my orders and will carry them out to the best of my ability. It is worth fighting through minor discomforts both physically and mentally.

Whatever time I have left in this life, for as long as blood pumps though my heart, I will live each day to its fullest. I will be dedicated to earning what members of the armed services do, and what a band of strangers did, to preserve my freedom. If I do not take advantage of the opportunities before me, I do not deserve them. No one else does either, if they do not embrace this concept.

I broke down and spilled tears in broad daylight as I thought about this. I was moved by the thought more than I was saddened. There's no crying in Texas, so I apologize to the natives of this state for mucking up their image. I was compelled to find time to write down my feelings, another taboo for this area.

Almost in montage format, I replayed the memories I had watching the second tower crumble on television. I was viewing it from a Best Western hotel room in Cabo San Lucas, Mexico. The government put us up in it after 29 days straight of patrol duties. We had just taken a break from the rocky, blue carpet ride the previous night.

I thought of the photographs I'd later see in Time Magazine of desperate men and women jumping to their death so as not to be engulfed in flames. These were someone's fathers, someone's mothers, and someone's grown children. Offices turned into infernos as smoke and toxic dust were inescapable. I began thinking about the film based on the events around United 93, when people just like us who never met before teamed together to do something heroic. I remember that final scene, camera view looking out of the window of the cockpit, as the earth came racing toward those doomed individuals. Anyone who has ever flown knows that is the greatest fear in manifest.

Being a young man with no combat experience of my own to draw from, I can't comprehend certain things. I would be dishonest if I claimed I could. In *Saving Private Ryan* a dying Tom Hanks tells Ryan to, "Earn this." When it goes back to present day, with Ryan looking over the tombstone of Hanks' character, he asks his wife if he has led a good life, and if he's a good man. I can never keep it together when I see or think about that scene as is evident from the watermarks on this notepaper.

My focus is restored. I know why it's important for me to do my part. I may have a predisposition for death crossing three states worth of desolate desert, but that is not the point. No gesture of mine will ever amount to the meaning behind it. Both the *what* and the *why* need to be understood. Since only a handful of people are aware of my walk, I can only hope that I can publish a good book and reach more people with the message I feel so driven to convey.

Lest I Ever Forget

Go Ready insect repellant has been my cologne of choice on this trip. The area where my bag meets with my back is saturated by sweat daily. I've witnessed mosquitoes pass me over and attack my monkey instead. I'm not jealous, just a little hurt.

After taking a short break to pull myself together, I was able to advance only a little further before sitting behind a commercial construction site. There was a problem. 290's service road, the one I've been walking, has no shoulder over a small stretch of bridge. The traffic was steady so I had to use caution. The creek was far too wide for me to jump from one bank to the other, with or without a 35-pound Monkey on my back. I'm not Neo from *The Matrix* just yet.

I contemplated ideas for solving the problem and test-ran them in my mind for a while. Either I have real shitty ideas or there was no good way to solve this dilemma. After a lot of stalling, I finally made a Comanche Run across the bridge. I am not a patient man. I find it to be boring, not to mention lazy.

There are dreadful amounts of hungry mosquitoes on this stretch. I had been slapping myself retarded as I attempted to squeeze a few more miles out of the day. What's worse, I just spoke to Bobby Glass. I should be heading toward San Antonio on I-10, not Austin on 290W. I have to find a way to remedy this. I don't want to waltz back into Houston's city limits. Building a fire there would be an express pass to a jail cell. I'm going to find a place nearby to camp tonight and work this fresh bit of nonsense out in the morning.

November 3rd: I had a nice fire last night behind a building that was still under construction. The workers were gone for the day, of course. There were piles of scrap 2X4 at my disposal. I drank from an outside faucet after filling my water bottle. It was a pleasant evening with no run-ins of any kind. I spent most of the day gathering highly misleading, and not at all similar, data from the locals. Directions having that much variance from one person to the next concern me, greatly. I ended up choosing one option from the bunch that I wanted to believe above the rest. *Find your truth amidst the lies.* I walked 290's service road going East this time. Just for the hell of it, or maybe so I could feel like a car, I made my way to the other side of the road. As I did, I found something of interest on the ground. There was a Harley-Davidson brand beanie lying in the short grass flush to the edge of the road's shoulder. The tags were still on it and it was perfectly clean. I picked up my unexpected gift from above, snapped off the tags and put it on. I never had a beanie that fit so well and looked so nice. No longer would I be as cold, which was inspiring, being that the evenings have been cooling off earlier. I'm losing my handsome tan here in Texas.

Barker-Cypress is where I had the bridge trouble. It's worse on this side due to overgrowth and passing water. I would need Gore-Tex supported boots and a machete to even consider this avenue. There would have to be a fair amount of luck on my side, as well. Who knows what this area is a natural habitat for? I'm thee intruder in their territory. Since either side were not options, I decided I'd try going straight down the middle of the divided highway. I walked across the eastbound lanes until I go to the grassy median and I trekked the downward slope between the two bridges. I was a man amongst giants as the concrete support pillars surrounded me. Judging by the debris, this is likely home to men who spend their day hustling honest people in an effort to provide for their disgusting drug habits. After the Coast Guard experience, where I was on drug interdiction missions, I always wanted to work for the DEA. I still do. Of course I wouldn't follow their rules either. I'd likely bust the assholes that have deals worked out with our government rather than their competition. I've witnessed it firsthand. We would spot a vessel that was officially identified as a mule by Intel, and we weren't able to touch it. JTAF-West would not give us authorization. Why do you think that is? It happened on more than one occasion. I thought we were trying to prevent the trade, not create a monopoly. It made me wonder why I was wasting 28 to 30 days straight, in the middle of the ocean, if we weren't even allowed to do our jobs. It was difficult enough for me to find a girlfriend back then. Being gone more than I was in port only aggravated my efforts.

"It's a good thing it's still daylight," I said aloud to myself. I didn't want to be there, with a bag full of goodies, when these retches returned to claim their sleeping bags and junk. As I approached the creek I saw that someone had carefully placed large stones across it, making a land bridge. Anyone who has ever gone hiking has seen this before. Depending on the mineral resources available I've seen them made from smooth, round sandstone to chunks of shale and granite. It was an easy run across the slick rocks and up the hill of the other bank. I emerged between traffic, beating a path in the itchy grass. I was standing a little taller, proud of my successful problem solving.

7:15pm: I'm taking a pit stop. I decided to abandon the service road and walk directly on 290. There's a nice, wide shoulder, making the environment for safe passage available. I traded up from the complete lack of a shoulder on the other road. I was walking in grasses that carry sharp, spiny green thorn-balls. They are vicious and caused me to make frequent stops as I tore them out of my flesh and off of my shoelaces. My legs look like an impressive work of horror film make-up art. There are scratches and cuts all over my shins and calf muscles.

November 4th, Election Day: People are always being encouraged to vote, exercise their rights, etc. They are never encouraged to research facts before making decisions, however. Mostly they do whatever the media, Hollywood, myspace blogs, and MTV tell them to.

    If someone has no knowledge of track records, positions on key topics, policy, and all the other things that a selection should be based on, by all means, stay the fuck home! Voting is a right and it should not be taken lightly. It's not a social event where you get to feel like you're finally part of the popular crowd of kids. That's what it's become through generations of bastardization. Uneducated voters, lets just call them *liberal democrats* for the lack of a better term, have about as much of a right to be at a ballot box as I do on someone else's Honeymoon.

    When people make hasty decisions at the horse track it adjusts the odds for everyone else's wager. The mobs of $2 betters set the numbers. In something as important as an election, a $2 bet should be considered an act of treason. They had little invested, and the outcome truly matters not, as far as they are concerned. All these actions cause are the introduction of free radicals, of chaos, into the equation. It steals logic away from the outcome. I'd never tell anyone not to vote. What I am saying is if you do, you have a responsibility to know what the fuck you're doing. If you don't want to be misrepresented for the next 4 years, it's probably worth the time to collect the facts. Those who don't put forth the effort are revoking their right to complain about their elected official, later. It should be everyone's goal that an official be elected by the TRUE VOICE of the people, and not by a chaotic infection, with no consideration for what they are doing and no accountability for their actions. The passive, liberal socialist is more of an anarchist than even they realize.

Day 32: Who knew? I thought Governor Palin for Vice President would have been twice as sexy as Dick Cheny. I'm a little disappointed she won't be in the public eye as much anymore. Alas, it was no small victory for Mr. Obama and Smokin' Joe Biden. There's nothing like getting your ass slapped to the ground while trying to sneak in a quick lay-up is there, McCain?

Let's not forget about RON PAUL. If the media tries to make you forget, that should be your first indication you're being manipulated and screwed. The man was a Constitutionist. That to me is far more important than selecting which animal I want sending the youth to their deaths; a donkey or an elephant.

"Change" for the sake of being different is as pointless and useless as alternative fuel hype. If it's "change" with a purpose, is that purpose valid? Can it be accomplished? Sometimes even a great idea can be sought after through ineffective strategies. I hope just the promise of "change" isn't what so many were sold on before understanding how this proposed "change" was to come about. Apparently Yoda was the Obama-Biden campaign advisor. All the podiums Obama made his speeches at had signs on them reading, "Change We Need." It didn't say, "We Need Change," or even "*The* Change We Need." Wisdom in the face of dyslexia: that is what the Obama campaign stood for. What's the adage? "With Yoda on our side, who could be against us?"

A Message to President-Elect Obama: Congratulations, you got the job! Now come January it will be time to have to do it. I hope there isn't a disorganized, "holy-shit" scramble resulting in loss of focus, confidence, and effectiveness. You weren't hired to be a celebrity, although that seems to be how the American people like to choose their officials. There's an extremely important task-at-hand. Burying yourself too deep in a pile of advisors will do nothing, but water down any uniqueness your personality and style could bring. If one is told how to think and act, are they not puppets? Be careful of the tendency to give into such pressures, thereby reducing your own power and influence.

I side with the American people. This seems to be what the majority of them wanted, but when has anyone *really* known what they want? Regardless, it is your responsibility to represent the People, not just speak on their behalf. The right way is achieved by listening to them. The wrong way is to blindly act without their input. Ego tends to make the latter all too popular. The virtues set forth when this country was forming through writings such as the Federalist Papers, and Thomas Paine's "Common Sense" should be the only virtues of concern. No special interests, no backroom handshakes, and certainly no secret alliances or support should attack the integrity of our country's ability to operate and succeed. This is a country intended for the people. Mess it up and I promise you, We *will* take it back.

Hopefully you will choose your cabinet much like Lincoln did. The man took everyone who hated and doubted him and gave them jobs. He didn't surround himself with a group of less qualified "yes" men. He selected the best for the job, regardless. As Leslie Neilson said in *Airplane,* I just wanted to say to you, 'Good luck, and we're all counting on you.'"

CRAZY RON & the RED RANGER: The heading reads like the name of just another cheap team of radio shock jock personalities whose refusal to admit they emulate the Godfather of the practice, Howard Stern, ultimately leads to their downfall. This was a man, however. This is the story of my interaction with Crazy Ron and his Ford Ranger.

Usually *crazy* follows a certain set of boundaries and has similar characteristics from one form to another. Once established, its nature reveals itself and truly dangerous behavior can be identified from that of the less invasive "barking." In most cases when you meet a *crazy* person, you learn quickly just how far you can push them before you're riding in the "red" with potentially explosive consequences. With Ron, there was hardly a clear line.

Ron was a rare, unique breed. As I sat in front of, you guessed it, a Wal*Mart, Ron approached me with an intrigued look on his face. It was as if his thin smile was holding back millions of gallons of dam water. Engaged in conversation with a guy who parked his Harley practically on top of the bench, Ron walked up to the both of us.

I was walking back from a Famous Footwear location after having discovered my latest obsession I could not afford, a pair of Air N' Sight III's by Nike. I tried them on and they would be perfect for the continuation of my quest. I made a note of the name, and size that fit in the hopes of acquiring them in the near future. As I ate my Slim Jim dinner I noticed a red and black Harley right near my Big Green Monkey. I quickened pace to assess the scene. Luckily there was no damage to the monkey, so I sat back down and continued eating my grease stick. If I leaned forward I would have bumped my head on the motorcycle's shiny gas tank. I didn't care. I was in snack food Zen at the moment. Had I witnessed an old lady bouncing off the hood of a speeding car, I would have been indifferent to it… Unless, of course, she was passing out free Slim Jims at the time.

Refueling is important when plans call for long-term exertion. This was my way of mustering up the required energy and determination for such a task. I had a four-mile walk through a mostly Mexican, urban setting before meeting up with I-10.

The proprietor of said Harley came out of the store and lit up a cigarette. I didn't see any grocery bags, so it's safe to assume his purchase was related to that item burning 4 inches from his nose. Seeing me on the bench, the man with jet-black hair and a white t-shirt apologized for his intrusion. Hearing him speak broke me from my food hypnosis. The man sounded like a nervous Elvis Presley. He introduced himself as Shawn, and asked me what the Big Green Monkey was for.

I'm not from Texas, but if you're going to be anything, you may as well be a Texan. At least they are a proud bunch. The eccentrics, or artistic, creative type are more like this man Shawn and less like some Tinker Bell fashion designer from NYC or Hollywood. Although I despise country music and view it as a virus infecting progressive evolution of the human race, I do like Rockabilly from this area. The Reverend Horton Heat would be a good example. Shawn's appearance reminded me of of it. He was very polite, and to hear the way he talked was a novel delight in itself. He wished me luck, as most people do upon hearing my plans, and sat down on his bike. I handed him a card and told him he could visit the website.

Ron came up to us as he was exiting the Great Wal's magnificent automatic doors. He stood quietly, with that contorted smile and patiently waited for Shawn and I to wrap up our dialogue. Shawn nodded to Ron as he speed off into the evening. "There goes Elvis incarnate," I said under my breath as I waved goodbye.

I was now facing a character whose Hawaiian board shorts, and 24 Hour Fitness t-shirt ensemble was indicative of someone who makes hasty decisions. Combined with his wild yellow-white hair and eyeglasses he could have been mistaken for a science professor out for a swim. "You're doin' a little walkin' I hear?"

"Yeah, to California, eventually." I stood up and shook his hand, "I'm Daniel."

"Well Daniel, I'm Ron. Over there, that's my red ranger. If you'd like a ride somewhere I'd be happy to take ya. I only live a few blocks from here."

Ron was the type of person who got kicks out of social interaction. He was a hootin' hollerin' Texan that would say anything to anyone just to get a high. He was probably a genius somewhere beneath all the absurdity. He got off on making others terrified and uncomfortable with his presence. It was a joke for him and most people were so uptight that they didn't understand he was putting them on. So he fucks with them to see what they're made of. Ron's a busy man. He hasn't a moment to spare on someone not worth his time. I learned this when he spotted a Spanish lady collecting shopping carts and he called out to her, "Emilio! Emilia! Emilio Estevez!" He was in the middle of asking me what was in my Big Green Monkey when the distraction won him over. He decided to harass this woman. "That's my ex-wife, Rosa," Ron said.

"She's not much for conversation. Do you know how far I am away from I-10?"

"North or South? Because each way is just as far, Ha-Hooo!" Ron was entertaining himself.

"I-10 runs East and West," I corrected him.

"Well, since when? When'd they change it, Hee-hoo!" He bent back so far I thought his spine was going to fold on him. He looked like a werewolf howling at a full moon. "It's about, I don't know, four miles... Unless they moved it." I had no choice but to take a ride with this guy, if only to further understand his dementia. The last two days I spent backtracking for a total of over 48 miles of unnecessary walking. A four-mile trip in the Red Ranger was well earned.

He told me to get my bag ready and wait for him to pull the Red Ranger around. As he was approaching me, creeping up a lane of the parking lot, he stuck half his body out the window and shouted, "Are you ready, yet? Let's ride, Wooo-wee!"

I was too busy laughing on the inside to feel embarrassed or self-conscious. This character might be a lunatic, but at least he's upbeat. I lugged my cumbersome bag by one strap and set it in his truck. He began slapping his door as if it were a horse or a plump woman's ass. I got into the passenger side and looked at him a moment. Ron's the type of guy you just come straight out and ask, "You aren't going to kill me, right?"

He laughed wildly and shouted, "I got no more room! Never shoulda got in that business!" He fell a little short of putting me at ease.

Ron tried to convince me to go to his house and get stoned with him. I declined the offer, sighting my need to maintain my motivation, which he agreed. We were moments from where he told me he'd bring me when he took a surprise right-hand turn into a development. I asked him where we were going as I took the knife out of my pocket and slowly, quietly unfolded it. I held it where he couldn't see it, between the passenger door and myself, and I was ready for a showdown.

"I want to show you where I live n' case you change your mind and want to hang out." Could this be how I die? Or was Ron genuinely lonely and in need of a friend? I couldn't relax my defense until I was certain of his true intentions. After a tense, but short cruise through a neighborhood, we arrived at a circular road and a modest, but well maintained house. He slowed the truck to a stop and pointed out the window. "This is it. If you decide you need a rest or a shower, I'm usually here." He got the truck moving again, and we left the way we came. I folded my pocketknife and put it back in my pocket feeling a little guilty for my suspicious reaction. He dropped me off less than 2 miles from where I-10 was. It was a great help, because the street scene that I would have had to travel through looked a bit rougher than I cared to deal with. Here I was almost ready to gore someone who was just trying to be nice. It doesn't matter how many hitchhikers he's eaten. What matters is how I was treated.

Thanks for the ride, Ron. And thank you for not killing me.

God is everywhere. The smokescreen that traditional society blinds us with, coupled with the distractions of the rat race block this truth from ever penetrating our conscious thoughts. It is quite obvious to me having cleared the air of this ignorant debris. I've encountered things on my journey I value as daily miracles evident of a guiding hand. God was there. I felt a presence, and I had a friend to keep me company. I knew I could trust this feeling, so long as I kept true to my better judgment. Samuel L. Jackson said it best as the character, Jules Winfield, "Whether He turned Coke into Pepsi, or help me find my fucking car keys..." God was there. "You don't judge these things based on merit."

8pm to the "ish" power: I've made it to I-10. I'm staring at it from a tiny park illuminated by a single streetlight. My foot and back are uncooperative members of my battalion at present. I have a discoloration on the bottom of my foot, likely a cocktail, two parts fluid and one part blood. The sore had formed deep in my foot underneath an old blister I had drained days ago, leaving loose flesh along its perimeter. I can tell I'm overtired the way my words are spilling onto the paper. I will rest here a bit, beneath my chosen tree, and pray the ants are unmotivated tonight. For now I will only gaze at the course ahead of me. Locals call it a Feeder Road, because it feeds traffic to the Interstate. I call it a service road because it serves the main road, and it is the location of all the commerce, or services. In the more wholesome days of my grandfather's youth, he'd have called it a Tow Path. I like his definition best.

<u>Day 32-34</u>: The evening was peaceful and I slept for two solid hours undisturbed. It was the most relaxing sleep I've had in weeks, hotel nightmares included. The rest of the night was off and on, 20 minutes here, 10 minutes there. That has become the norm since this trip began. By 5:30am I was motivated enough to want to wash up somewhere and begin my day. If my left foot deceives me, I might just cut the fucker off. I'd hate to be grumpy this early and let it infect the rest of my day with negativity.

I walked alongside I-10 as planned, until I reached Gessner Rd. There I went on a hunt for a place to scrub-shower, perhaps *borrow* some food from a sleepy grocery conglomerate, and find a park where I could stab into my foot a bit and then sterilize it.

At a gas station, a local Slim Jim Terrorist told me I could find a library a few miles in the direction I was walking.

Slim Jim Manifesto: To all the gas station and convenience store owners of this great nation, BE ADIVSED! Slim Jims are made from MEAT! What do you think happens to the integral cell structure of meat when you allow it to slow-bake for countless days on end? Do you think it's somehow impervious to such attacks, sustaining its freshness in the face of brutal assault? With this treatment could it ever be as delicious as the distributor and *God* intended it to be? The answer is; it dries and mummifies the skinny, brown bastard!

Why then, do so many storeowners insist on displaying their Slim Jim rack in front of windows or in the direct path of sunlight? The windows only intensify these rays concentrating them, and making them more harmful to innocent meat sticks.

It is criminal to alter the taste, quality standards, and freshness of a product that the distributor has worked to create a homeostatic environment for. Nothing is more disappointing than walking away from a purchase, anxiously anticipating the first bite, the first "Snap" into the product and... No "Snap!" Instead we're treated to a rubbery texture and an unpleasant discharge of grease into our throats. It's similar in physical properties to a piece of pepperoni that's been tortured in a microwave.

I appreciate the fact that the majority of convenience storeowners hail from countries where it was socially acceptable to hang dead chickens and goats out for display, all day, in the hot desert sun. When they go back to visit they can do the same with their Slim Jims, but not here. This is America. *We* do things a little differently here. Embrace it! If your country was so terrific, why did you ever leave it? We can fix that. Here's your plane ticket, have a great trip, and the peanuts are free.

I can put up with a lot of injustice in this world. I've been beaten up by police in a precinct where my head was used to batter open the doors. Bullies used to pick fights with me everyday in school. Just don't ask me to swallow substandard practices when it comes to my favorite snack food. Hold you nothing sacred?

I'm not asking anyone to go above and beyond their call of duty as proprietors. It's not too much to ask they exercise a little common sense and stop cooking Slim Jims and melting candy bars before they reach my face. This is **snack food terrorism**!

I'm confident that most would see this message as a public service. If they were aware of the money they were losing, they'd probably stop cooking their own merchandise and begin using their heads. Move food products containing ingredients such as meat and chocolate out of the sun. Together we *can* make a difference. We stand as one voice, working to build a better tomorrow... For snack food enjoyment.

I ended up on a bus stop bench shortly after, praying for my foot not to explode in my shoe. I was offered a ride from a local. This large Mexican-American was driving a beat-up Suburban, and had the voice of a chipmunk. I only had 4,000 feet to travel before reaching the library, but I accepted the offer. I'm about to perform an amputation on myself rather than deal with this pain any longer. Imagine if you will, the sensation of air being pumped directly into your foot at a rate that rivals a tire pump. There's a release, but then it seems to fill up with more air, each throbbing interval. That's what's going with the bottom of my foot. If I pause from walking for a moment, the next step feels like my foot is splitting lengthwise.

Juan is the man who gave me a ride to the library. I might take refuge at his place for the evening. He offered after having seen the discomfort painted all over my face. I've been carrying on with injuries rather than giving them proper attention and time to heal. I'm dragging my agony out longer than necessary. I will not allow myself to walk like a cripple the rest of the way. It makes me feel pathetic. I can only imagine how it must look.

In Florida I can get away with carrying a big, crazy stick around wherever I go. I'm glad I didn't do that here in Texas. I doubt I would have had as many opportunities to "break the ice" in some of the more crucial conversations that led to needed advice, directions, and assistance. I left Mitch in the truck, and there he will remain until Bobby Glass and I meet up. Random acts of kindness and generosity have kept me going and are well appreciated.

The real test is yet to come. I will not accept any rides as I travel through the three desert states to my final destination on the sands of Venice Beach. Semi-survivalist efforts will intensify to all out survival strategy as I make this climate and terrain transition. I'm not only concerned with the drastic temperature variations from night to day, but also with rattlesnakes and scorpions. Rattlesnakes are not something you want to step on when leaving your tent for a 3:00AM piss. Scorpions were a terrible band and I don't respect their genre. Do sandstorms occur in US states? Food and water will be harder to come by and I'm told people need these things. I doubt there are a lot of outlets to charge my phone or libraries for updating my website in the Mojave.

No amount of money or social status is protection from the dangers found in the desert. All the nonsense people place artificial value on as they scurry around their little rat maze is useless in these lands. Rattlesnakes don't care if your key chain has a Saturn or a BMW logo on it. You are fair game. I've become aware of how foolish the pursuit for possessions is, and it's difficult to fathom going back under the ether. I'm convinced that a life of real purpose is a separate path from the one most of society walks. Social and economic issues are problems of people with something to lose. The more one has the more they have at stake. This is why neurosis is so prevalent. It's an anxious and desperate way to live.

Before heading out from El Paso, I'll make sure I can tie the best snares this world has to offer. I'll prepare and plan, for these skills come natural to me. The road ahead leads to the most barren of this country's wastelands. I'd be a fool not to respect that.

The library was crowded, so I locked my Big Green Monkey to the bike rack of outside. I think it would be amusing to have a car alarm for my backpack. I could drop the bag down like I did, and secure it. Then, as I walk away I'd hold the remote over my left shoulder and press the "arm" button. That gratifying, familiar sound, "Eee-Ooh-Eee" would resonate in the air. That should cause more than one head to be scratched in confusion.

I hobbled across the street to a Whataburger restaurant. At this time of day the place is filled with assistance walkers, blue-toned hair perms, and liver spots. I'm not sure what senior citizens see in places like this and Mc Donald's, but there are countless numbers of them every morning, from my old hometown all the way to East Texas, at least. If this place follows similar practices as Mc Donald's there's a coffee discount offered to silverbacks. Make no mistake about it. This is *their* hang out. They even have clicks like those found in school lunchrooms. If I live long enough I may unlock the mystery behind the attraction. I too, may spend eight to ten hours each day sipping bad coffee, staring at and shuffling newspapers, and mingling with my fellow fossils. I don't think the sum of my actions in life will ever add up to that rotten outcome, but I'm still very young in comparison. What the hell do I know?

Politics, world issues, and the dreaded *opinion* on each topic weigh heavy in the Whataburger air. Typically, the discussions are thin, and ill informed. Often they are over-simplified to the point of absurdity. Choice sound bytes like, "housing crisis," and "bank bail-out" are extracted from context and whirled around the room until they've lost all purpose and intent. They are constantly recycled into their conversations until they become diluted. Often the statements made by the fossils indicate that they can't see beyond their little nook to the grander picture. As long as it works in their concept of the world, the only concept they concern themselves with, they're satisfied. Their belief structures are based on a unilateral vantage point. They're all crammed in a little rowboat wearing yellow rain slickers and shouting at one another when someone begins to rock it. This breeds ridiculous and bizarre theories as to how *all* things should be managed.

I made it back over to the library to find my monkey engaged in conversation with a crow. I called Juan and made it official. I accepted his generous offer and will be staying with him until Bobby Glass returns from his Mexican exploitations. Finally I will have some real time to heal and to write. First order of business will be to shower and then stab my foot with my Gerber folding knife until I dig out whatever cancer is eating away at me. Hopefully, I can avoid further exterior medical hang-ups this trip. Juan and his son don't live far from the library, according to his directions, making this is an ideal situation. God is in everything and everywhere. I'll repeat it as much as I feel I have to.

Juan swung by the library and dropped me off money to use toward picking us up some beer. Is this heaven?

<u>Day 35</u>; WTF, (Over): At any given time a man can find himself playing roles of either the predator or the prey in nature, the demon or the angel. Life has moveable parts like that of a chess game, and here, strategy is the only saving virtue. This is good news for an asshole like myself. Up until now, I've heard others spout off countless times about *patience*. I resemble nothing of this quality, but I have plenty of ambition when it comes to playing the game. There are distinct, opposing sides, and any negative space can be an interface for battle. Sometimes it is unclear which side you represent until the cannon smoke dissipates, and you're left with a view of the aftermath.

Lately when I dream I see a depiction of hell. I see demons interacting with humans and making them into beasts like themselves with tools such as temptation, desire, and greed. I see them working to acquire my soul and their maddening frustration over not already having it. Rationalization is a path to evil in most cases. Excuses, reasons, best intentions, they all service the growing Legion. Doubt is their best selling item. It's the plague of mankind responsible for more lost loves, lost faith, and lost interest in fighting the good fight.

Make no mistake. Hell isn't some concept or place only existing in the imagination. Hell is right here. It's all around us. It's in our hearts and on the tips of our tongues. Most of us are drones, so detached from the *real* that we are manipulated by these desires. We can't trust our conscience if *conscience* is constantly in upheaval. It changes so often, how do we know if we're listening to our id, ego, or superego at any given time? We choose our truths and our values by what is most favorable to us at the time. Evil has an easy time at guiding us in its direction. It could be something as simple as being discourteous and selfish, to physically harming someone. You may say things to a loved one you don't really mean, but you felt justified in doing so. Why? What desire empowered that ugly part of you with a voice? We think we're self-righteous, but really we're fools playing right into the hands of the Great Deceiver. Every moment of existence is part of a grand test. It is a power struggle for human souls. You can be convinced you're different, that you're saved. You're not. We wouldn't still be in this dump if we were finished with our test. It makes you rethink the adage, "Only the good die young," doesn't it?

I find myself playing the reluctant role of gatekeeper on this journey. I am not saved, and I am not doomed. I am able to walk in both lanes just as I can along the divided highway. I'm not pure enough to go any higher, and so far I've resisted all the attempts evil has made to infect my soul. Maybe this is my purpose. Maybe I'm supposed to shake people from their slumber and let them take the next step on their own. How long will I be required to do this, I wonder? I know that I am willing to do whatever is asked of me. I have love in my heart and it has protected me in more ways than anyone would believe. Because of that, I will do what I must, what I can, and what I feel I should, forever. I never want to lose touch with the warmth I feel loving my dearest Alice, my family, and this life, whatever it means. I am a warrior. I am Daniel. I sense that most of evil's army would rather focus on easier targets than waste extra effort on me. They'll scowl and hiss for now, but the showdown is yet to be scheduled. With this time, I must take advantage of my position and do as much good as I can. What better protective shield, than a guy no one wants to deal with? Whether I drag as many as I can off the battlefield, or I slap them in the face and wake them up to the war itself, I must do my part or my own demise may follow. Of course, this was a feeling derived from several nights of dreams. It could just mean I needed more water before bed, or that I should play the lotto.

I'm going to make a t-shirt with Christopher Lloyd's character from *Back to the Future* on it. I'll probably go with a frame of him with his hands raised. The shirt will say, "Jigga-watt?!"

I had a whole set plan of what I was going to write about and now my emotions are all *out-of-whack* because of my ex-fiancé's efforts to break me. This is a sickness. She's displaying the characteristics and properties of a Succubus. Everything that I took into the relationship was devoured, consumed. If I didn't love her so much I wouldn't feel this hurt. I guess that shows I'm on the right track as a person.

Matters of the heart are my greatest weakness. What you see is what you get with me. I'm not guarded, or frightened to be myself. Unfortunately, that leaves me vulnerable to attack, as well. Alice knows things about me others do not. She tries to belittle me and embarrass me by broadcasting this information when she's upset. It doesn't work. I am not ashamed to face the reality of who I am. There's nothing all that bizarre or terrible to fear exposure of. It's all gone into the same kettle that produced the rich soup of my soul, today. Watching her lose control of her anger in a malicious effort to ruin me is what is so upsetting. To see how badly she wants me to suffer is the part that is unbearable. This goes deeper than any cold morning, and aching body. I will not allow for anything, ANYTHING, to pull the plug on this quest. It is in my control and it's over when I say it's over. I will use the anguish and recycle it as determination to keep driving that metaphoric thorn into the sides of those who continue to take issue with my decisions. I'm through fighting. Negativity fought with negativity is an ancient, fool's game.

Enough of that... There's a far greater issue to address

Cheap Fried Chicken Scourge: *The downfall of Western Civilization*

Certain establishments are warning signs, symbols identifying a bad part of town. If you ever find yourself sitting on a plastic lawn chair looking over the black, painted, steel railing of an apartment complex's second floor balcony, then absorb the surroundings. If there's an automobile rim shop as your next-door neighbor, refracting streetlight in majestic, hypnotic patterns into the night sky you may wish to take caution. This is typically a badge of less desirable neighborhoods. In my case, suspicion was further confirmed by the sight of a *Popeye's Chicken & Biscuits* across the street, diagonal to my position. If you happen by a street with a *Church's Chicken* on it, you better pray to God you're either heavily armed or you can run like a gazelle at moment's notice. One of the two qualities will be called on for certain. There's a *Church's Chicken* one block away in the opposite direction of the rim shop and *Popeye's*. I'm in the crosshairs of what the locals here call, "some bad shit."

Any restaurant that sells fired chicken at such a value is bound to attract all types, including the potentially lethal urban predators. I've seen *King of New York*, so I know what goes on. The sign should read, "Come for the Crispy Batter. Stay for the Double Homicide." There, children don't get crayons with their place settings. They get white chalk, so they can assist with outlining the bodies.

Is this to blame for the violence in the American ghettos? Do ghettos attract these businesses or do the corporations turn their surrounding neighborhood into a ghetto? Is fried chicken somehow linked to the increase in crime rate? Is it chemical?

It is irresponsible to sell fried chicken as cheap as *Church's* does. Who can resist this golden, crispy batter? They're asking for trouble. It's too convenient, leading me to believe this may very well be part of some evil, hidden agenda. There just might be a Fried Chicken Conspiracy!

Church's isn't the only player in the game. *Popeye's* does their part to deliver poultry at affordable prices, as well. I've also seen a KFC or two that hold a $4.99 All-You-Can-Eat feeding frenzy at predetermined hours of the day.

If such a conspiracy does exist, we're looking at an epidemic of truly massive proportions. If any of us hope to survive, we're going to need a team of heavily guarded scientists working around the clock on this. Lab technicians will need to examine crispy golden samples from all fried chicken establishments, including family-run businesses and testing them against a lab-fried, control group. It's the only way to determine whether the problem lies in the fried chicken itself, or if there's some corporate additive that brings about violent tendencies in the would-be consumer.

Perhaps there is some kind of tampering going on with certain, or all fried chicken corporations, as part of a secret **global domination plot**. Its soldiers are innocent ghetto men, women, and children with stomachs full of inexpensive demon chicken, possessing them to carry out the bidding of their favorite, convenient food stop. We'll not know how widespread this problem is, or who's involved, until all testing is completed on the samples. I implore those officials, with the power to act, not to take this lightly. Act now before it's too late! Our very own children could be next. We'll find them in their rooms, candles lit, praying to the disembodied head of Colonel Sanders on their grease stained chicken buckets all because we saw a bargain and couldn't resist.

Day 36-38: Juan received some painful news, today. He was informed that his nephew was hit by a school bus while walking home. The kid is now in the hospital with complex internal injuries including a collapsed lung and broken ribs. A similar event occurred in 2006, killing one of Juan's sons. I was unaware how common these types of accidents are. I guess I was sheltered living in cow and pasture town, USA.

That same year Juan lost his daughter to illness, and his wife to suicide as a result of the two previous events. I see now why this man was so sympathetic to a limping, young man with a Big Green Monkey on his back. It's a way for him to feel needed, to feel like a father, again. I'm sure an event this close to the one that killed his son is opening the gates of suppressed aguish for him.

While I was making huge paychecks for myself at the mortgage company, feeling like a big shot, and hoping for management offers having just helped the corporate machine open their first satellite branch, Juan was chaining himself to the local railroad tracks in an attempt to reunite with his beloved family. If not for the courageous acts of the good people Juan worked with at Kroger's Grocery, Juan too, would have met his demise. Their quick response got him off the tracks minutes before he would have been reduced to chunky Kool-Aide. The local Samaritans called the train station and urged them not only to switch the track's path, but also to notify the conductor of the urgency to slow to a stop. I'm glad they did.

There's no telling what I would do in the wake of such tragedy. If I lost my brother, my sister, Alice who's giving me nothing but reasons to want to dislike her, I could have easily been him. Juan is not a bad guy for having a heart. This should not be seen as a negative, and that is why I hate Catholics who lecture how suicide is a ticket to Hell. It's not always a selfish act. The good in the man, his love, his broken heart, is what brought him to those tracks. If anything, it is evident of the man's humanity.

It is a pleasant stay in this apartment. I am truly grateful for it. I've taken more detailed care of my feet. The wounds could still open, if encouraged. For now, however, I am getting healthier and stronger each hour. I owe this opportunity to Juan, my new friend. It won't be forgotten, nor will the hours of Univision I've been subjected to.

Univision is one of many Spanish channels available in Texas. With Laredo, MX closeby, and the Rio Grande, and all that political nonsense not worth the time addressing, there's a demand for such services. This particular channel plays what can best be described as high definition, prime-time soap operas. Juan and his son love them. I can't understand what they're saying, but I pick up the body language. There's an abundance of exaggerated drama and crying going on in the fictitious lives of these ethnic characters.

The women are very easy to look at, with heaving breasts squeezed to death in low cut blouses. So, I guess there's a little something for everyone. What intrigues me the most are the television commercials for familiar products and services done the

Latin-American way. You'd assume for the sake of cost, they'd be the same commercials, only dubbed over in the appropriate language. That's not the case. The market is apparently large enough for companies like Macy's and Rooms to Go to devote a budget toward creating original advertising just for this audience. Fascinating! I've watched enough Univision to where I'm left wanting more at the end of each program's cliffhanger.

I took a small hit off a blunt on a side street from where Juan works yesterday. I was walking my happy ass to where I was told I could find a Wal*Mart, not knowing that I was in gangland. A real, live skin-headed gangster walked up to me on the sidewalk with the blunt in his hand and asked me if I had a light. Immediately I reached in my left pant pocket and retrieved a device fitting of his request. He was a cool cat, the type you want to run into if you have to run into any of them. You could tell he sat in a position where he no longer had to prove his street credibility and was able to relax and be real. I liked him because I saw him as a guy playing the hand he was dealt, for better or for worse. His tattoos painted the scenes of the crucifix and the Virgin Mary. Some artist did beautiful work on the "praying hands" on the right side of his neck. He's a man who could be reasoned with, if it came down to it. He was about my height, which is ridiculously short. He offered me a hit and I took it. There are certain things you do to show your respect and to avoid arousing suspicion. For all I know he was a member of one of the many Mexican gangs carving their territory within these parts, but on a one-to-one basis he was a man like myself just going on with his day. That single hit had its grip on me for the next five hours. I drank two 40's in Juan's Suburban, having retreated from my plan to go to the Wal*Mart. It was too far away and I didn't want to be stranded had I come back too late.

Friday night was Laundry Night in little Mexico. Juan and I were waiting for clothes to finish their cycle, so we could get back to our Univision programs. We were about 9 blocks or more from his house, which was odd because we passed several other Laundromats before reaching this one. He explained we were driving almost ten minutes away because we could get the clothes done for 25 cents less per load. It hadn't occurred to him that he was spending more in gas just to save that quarter. We barely spoke. I think we were both under hypnosis from the turning drums in our respective dryers. We never even ironed out a plan for the coming day.

<u>November 11<u>th</u>, Veteran's Day</u>: Daniel, the patriotic, punk rock nomad would appreciate all who read this to take a moment and reflect on the sacrifices made by the brave.

It's time I step up to the plate and be a man, again. Alice, whether she knows or cares, has been with me every step of the way. She is in my heart and on my mind at all times. I have been unfair. I haven't really extended the benefit of the doubt to her. Her surface hatred is due to the fact that she loves me, at least, that is what I need to believe for now. She feels abandoned. I know this because apparently she's been discussing her feelings with my parents. What woman of deceitful, evil gains would bother talking to my family? If she was truly up to something with another guy, wouldn't she distance herself? It could be a clever plot to make me look like a bad guy to everyone I love, giving me nothing to go back to. I just can't believe I'd have her that wrong. The fact remains, I should have been more sensitive and validated her emotions, rather than arguing my case to the contrary. When she ended our engagement I was working off of self-preserving mechanisms in an effort to limit my own collateral damage. I've been going about things in my old way—the wrong way.

There are a million qualities that led me to fall in love with her. Looking back, I think all she wanted was Me. I felt I needed to solve everything and pay for more than I could. In an effort not to burden her or the children I left in hopes she would have an easier time at things. I missed her point from the very beginning. I am not above getting on my hands and knees and begging for her forgiveness. We both made mistakes, but we can't let that govern the rest of our lives. Forgiveness and acceptance need to be exercised.

Did the bad guys win?

Any fool can radiate with artificial importance wearing a nice suit and a Blue Tooth. Try that in the Suburban Jungle. Here, I speak softly and carry a big stick, literally.

Don't get the wrong idea regarding the nature of select journal topics. I am no longer anti-establishment, nor am I against society in any way. I love people so much that I want to see if they'd do things any different if they had my point of view on things. This exercise most of us are engaged in isn't the only game in town. I'm coming from a refreshing approach for the purpose of understanding my role in this world. I'm not Shane. I'm not here to ride off, half-dead, into the sunset. This is a temporary state, an experiment where I'm collecting as much raw data as possible in the hopes that once examined, it will enhance me as a person. Going back to the bare root of things can only help strengthen my character and show me what I'm made of. I appreciate what we have at our disposal in the modern world. I could use a little music from time to time on these long walks. I pose this question: Wouldn't it be nice to feel the childish thrill and fascination with things adults take for granted? Is there not some priceless innocence found in that state of being worth tapping into?

I was a hard working member of the rat race. I take much pride in what I produce coming from the old school of values. I was taught that the results of your work are a reflection of who you are. I love recognition just as much as the next go-getter. I hunger for success.

The values lost when lifestyle slowly shifted from survival to convenience, notice I didn't say, "evolved," had practical use in today's world. This is my opportunity to absorb this information and the lessons it teaches like an eager sponge. I'm gaining firsthand wisdom. This is better than any book I could read in a safe, household atmosphere. My goal is to someday learn all that I have yet discovered. I want to relearn it through experience rather than accept someone else's *truth*. I am appreciating things without the filter of preconception. For a writer, a fresh take on recognizable subject matter is crucial to existence.

I must confess I love the way the Big Green Monkey feels on me. It's a lot of work, but everything worth doing is. Rest assured I have every intention to reunite with Alice, my true love. I want to see my parents, my brother and sister, everyone. I was called to duty, so I had to go. Everything in my life up to the day I left had prepared me for that moment. It may never have been the right thing to do for anyone else, but my pieces of the puzzle came together that way.

"If I turn into another
Dig me out from under what is covering the better part of me
Sing this song
Remind me that we'll always each other
When everything else is gone…"

Incubus, *Dig*

Flexible Plan: Formless Form

There has been need for a reevaluation of present standings. The plan, after leaving Juan's home in Houston, was to catch a ride with Bobby Glass to the west end of Texas, El Paso. There I would be working for Bobby in an effort to raise the required capitol for desert supplies, and enough to send Alice to help with storage fees.

I had a feeling, but I wasn't aware just how strongly Bobby was opposed to my walk. He even packaged the offer with the words, "So you can make it out of the desert alive." I figured there was an understanding.

Fort Stockton, and the Devil's attempt to claim another hopeful soul

The devil takes all forms, none more deceiving than in the face of a man who's already earned your trust. Bobby Glass didn't arrive to pick me up that chilly morning in Houston. It looked like him. It drove his truck, but the man who I sat next to on that ride had a new agenda, foreign to my previous experience. Pompous Pilot did his very best to infect me with doubt once we reached the Executive Inn at Fort Stockton. He told me my book was ill conceived, that I'm not a writer, and that I should quit the walk.

He went so far as to suggest that I leave Alice, and never look back.

After eavesdropping on a conversation I was having on my mobile phone with Alice, Pompous made the comment, "That doesn't sound like it's over at all." It was said in a very negative, bitchy tone. He sat with his laptop on the tiny desk afforded us in our room. The rest of the night he had a permanent grimace etched on his face, complaining about the television, the food he bought, and everything else of low consequence. It appeared this force was looking to eliminate all feelings of hope, optimism, and positive energy.

That night I dreamt Pompous was the devil, chasing me through the desert with the assistance of a small town mob. I found myself in a desperate scramble for my life as I ducked behind nondescript homes in a trailer park atmosphere. In dreams, there can be an extreme feeling sensed that supercedes the course of events. One may find himself in a benign setting, but feel afraid. Other times it's more accurately paired with the situation. Sheer terror is the best way to describe what I had felt that night. It was all too vivid and I knew if I were caught that would be the end of me in all realms of consciousness. I managed to evade the torch burning locals and Pompous through an agonizing series of narrow escapes. I took the dream for what it was, a message. I am on the right track and this negative energy has found me and is trying to devour my very soul. It's attempting to corrupt my heart and convince me to give up on true love. It wants me to forget about all the things I've learned and discredit them. The negativity and self-doubt were lifted by morning. God warned me last night and I took the hint. Although still in the presence of danger, I had already won the battle. There was Daniel amidst the lions once more.

By the time I was showered and packed, the overall vibe in the room was quite clear. The El Paso details were about to change. Unknown was the near future. If only I had Yoda on my payroll... We visited a nearby shack called the Steakhouse Restaurant. It was a silent occasion. Pompous Pilot's behavior was off. He was over dramatizing his interest in the local shit-print newspaper he used as a makeshift cubical barrier between us.

We drank bad coffee while he ate a disgusting breakfast. When my mind is ablaze, I rarely have a stomach for food. I could have used some brandy in my cup this morning. Alice was at the forefront of my mind. I missed her and the kids, and after recent events, I wanted nothing more than to run to her and throw my arms around her.

I learned through previous road talk that Pompous had undergone vanity surgery. He had a ring placed in his stomach, allowing only small amounts of food to be consumed at a time. If he eats too much, or if he eats the wrong thing, like breads, he'll be forced to vomit involuntarily. This particular slop wasn't agreeing with him, so he visited the bathroom a total of three times. What a life! If only he knew of the ancient practice of binge and purge. He could have done that without the cost of an expensive medical bill. When in Rome…

After this tortured display of his own weaknesses, I hopped back in the truck with a sense of relief. I should have been anxiety stricken wondering how I was going to reset my plans once Pompous broke the news. I was too high on the victory, having already mentally defeated the most dangerous of adversaries. Who was this man of flesh in comparison to that? I could handle just about anything at the moment. I sunk into the driver's side chair and felt like a king. All I had to concern myself with was the beautiful desert scenery. My mind wandered as I fantasized climbing just about every Mesa we passed on the road to El Paso. Pompous slept most of the way or fidgeted with his phone and laptop in frustration. This wasn't his day. It was mine. He saw the look of empowerment on my face, and like the rest of the demons, decided it wasn't worth losing the energy trying to defeat me.

Pompous contemplated what he thought would be my demise last night. Too much negativity and ancient, familiar vibes filled the last eleven hours, so I was happy when he fell asleep. It gave me a chance to really take in the scenery without a bitchy commentary. If I said, "Look at that horizon line, it's amazing," he'd pipe up about snakes or how boring the nothingness was. The frustrated devil, having failed in his attempt to crush my spirit, was now revealing himself before his final assault. His jokes were all about Jesus and God and I found them all to be offensive, or sacrificing creativity for shock value. One thing he didn't mention was the fact that a guy who worked as a carpenter in life ended up dead, nailed to two pieces of wood. If that's not irony I don't know what is. I lit four menthol cigarettes back to back just because I liked having the window open a crack, allowing in fresh air. I barely touched any of them to my lips.

Pompous Pilot wanted me to sell my soul, to cave. Unfortunately for him, he arrived late. It already belonged to God and Alice. It's in very loving, caring hands with both parties. I see no urgency to modify that, especially not for a lackluster job. It was never part of the original plan, anyway. The stint would have kept me away from my girl that much longer. I didn't begin this journey dependent on a stranger's ultimatum and it would be a quick recovery to say the least. My greatest weapons against these temptations have been the love in my heart and the belief in myself. If I betrayed them, I'd be deserving of a fate far worse than that of a flea market employee in El Paso.

When we got closer to our destination, Pompous took the wheel. He was setting the stage for the big event. As he announced his news I played along, pretending to be shocked and apologetic. He got the joy he wanted in thinking he just left me to die. Pompous Pilot dropped me off at a Great Wal of Mart of all places. This was a sign that everything was going to be alright. I left Mitch, the stick, in his truck and uttered, "Souvenir."

Pompous handed me a folded fifty-dollar bill and said, "This should get you nowhere. Call your family and have them get you out of this."

With one beer down, fate, luck, and God found me shortly after. I located a library and a park on Yarbrough. During the day I flagged down a bus driver and got some directions for navigating the town. I also gained valuable information regarding the limited scope of westbound routes should I head for the desert. I'm writing all of this from a Comfort Inn that I'm not a registered guest at. The library is closed, and besides, they don't have a continental breakfast. I'm only 123 pounds, but I can eat my weight in bagels with cream cheese. Besides, I get a thrill out of getting away with things, taking risks, and pushing situations to their limits.

101 Uses for a Porta-John: *The Great Yucca Park Swindle*

Those who enjoy the Sex Pistols will understand the reference made in the title. I was a day early for the library. I wonder if they're open on Veteran's Day. I find librarians to be a silly bunch. These leftwing types oppose the very idea of war, they don't fight in them, and yet they're first in line to benefit from a day designated to honor soldiers. Any excuse will do for time off. It's not like they keep demanding hours as it is.

I ate Church's Chicken! The clever bastards were waiting for me, with an all too convenient location across the street from my latest foxhole, Yucca Park. There was a 2-piece, dark meat combo for $2.69. Who could say "no" to such wise economics? It came with mashed potatoes and a biscuit. I didn't need a drink, because I had already procured a cheap 40-ounce bottle of *malt lovely* from the grocery store just behind them.

I sat at a picnic table in the park and watched as minions of paired, middle-aged speed walkers scurried about the paved walking path. It's pleasing to see so many health conscious people here, especially when I was about to tear apart a greasy mess of a lunch. I smoked a cigarette with exaggerated satisfaction just for their sake. I'm sure I appeared pretty corrupt to them, not to mention, like an asshole. If only they knew the endeavor at hand.

There's a possibility that the cynical behavior I displayed was due to the ingestion of contaminated fried chicken. After all, was I not the person who warned of the possible dangers of eating this brand? I'm not concerned with my safety, however. I've built up quite a resistance to evil.

The park walkers go around and around on the preset course. I'm fascinated by this behavior. Even when they have so-called "free time" this is what they choose. They have no ambition to use their energy to seek adventure. All walkers want to do is circle their cages and repeat the same motions, seeing the same scenery. That's about as stimulating as the last few Oliver Stone pictures.

The wind is irritating me as I try writing in this damn notebook. Should I go home for the holidays? Of course I *should*. I miss Alice and the kids, and seeing other children play in the park leaves me feeling empty inside. If I'm not there then I have lost the meaning of this quest. This is about the American Dream, about love for family and country. It's not about being blindsided by an ideal making me neglect those most important to me. Efforts of the brave afforded me opportunities to find love and experience freedom. If I don't exercise those rights in my own life, then I don't deserve to have them.

I've lost all support, from sponsors to hollow-made promises. I haven't the funds for food or proper supplies. To walk into the desert right now wouldn't be heroic or dignified. It would be suicidal and selfish. As optimistic and tough as I may be, certain practical measures need to be considered. No amount of "press forward" attitude toward adversity can change that.

With no income, the little amount of capitol I have will soon be diminished, leaving me in an ever-worsening position to handle the coming challenges. Supplies will be consumed and there is no restock in my foreseen future. I am not a slick, thief type. I can't get away with stealing anything besides computer time and crappy breakfasts. It's not fear that plagues me, but guilt. It just doesn't feel right, and a second's worth of hesitation can result in a mug shot. Alas, I'll never be seen with a giant crossbow stuffed in my pants.

Attempting to get a job out here would be a daunting task. There are plenty of "Help Wanted" signs. That's not the issue. I have no permanent residence, and no means to acquire even a temporary one. If I sought day labor, that still would leave me with the chore of finding a place to waste time between working hours. I can't stay around in the same areas being idle. The risk of being perceived as a vagrant is too great. All it takes is for someone to notice me around a lot. I don't hear too many good things about prison, especially in Texas. I'm told the authorities can hold a nomad like myself for thirty days, without further provocation. My Big Green Monkey would be arrested, too. He'd be doing time in his own way, spending his days in a secured locker somewhere in the "checkout" area of Hotel Jail.

If I had everything I needed, there would be no journal entry of this nature. I'd be on my way to New Mexico, already. I've always wanted to visit. I've been to Old Mexico, and I don't see how the sequel could possibly be worse than the original. My guess is it would be like comparing *Evil Dead II* to *Evil Dead I*.

Most of the details would remain the same, but it was obvious they had a larger budget to create the new version justly. They should have called it, "Mexico Redo," with an attached apology for the old one.

I'm eager to experience what lies ahead. Deserts have always fascinated me. Even if I couldn't find any peyote, I'm sure it would be quite rewarding. Jesus, remember him? He went out into the desert and had visions, was tempted by Satan, and was spoken to by God. That might be an average Saturday night where some people come from, but to me it's still an intriguing venture. I can't help but wonder if there *is* some mysterious, divine force out there with the power to enlighten man. Why else would Pompous Pilot do his best to stop me from going further? What was I not supposed to witness?

All things considered, jumping into shark infested waters as an injured fish is still just plain STUPID! This was never meant to be a suicide mission. There isn't a whole lot of inspiration found in a dead hero. It doesn't show too much promise to those who may have bought the rhetoric up to that point. I don't want to end this book, "This is the way to live… Woops, I'm dead." I'll leave the role of *martyr* alone for the time being.

So, *did* the bad guys win? I don't think so. If I didn't make it out alive, then sure, score one for the bad guys. I know a lot of places are given scary names and talked about in scary ways to keep people from wandering into them. What are they hiding? Is the path to enlightenment the best kept secret of the world, or is it just news to me? There's a very real possibility that for now I need to pick up my golf ball, spot it with a quarter, and come back when I have sufficient gear and funds to play the next hole. As Pompous said, "…Or they may discover your sun-bleached bones several years from now."

Last night was quite an excitement. The many hands of Vishnu produced powerful winds that were delivering chills straight to my bones. I made my way across the park where, from a previous usage, I was aware the porta-johns were pristine. Just in front of Yarbrough stood a duplex toilet apartment. Wouldn't you know there was a vacancy!

I chose the one to the right. "If the right hand deceives thee, flush it down." The interior was in rare, mint condition. Even the blue abyss was clean and floater-free. The toilet paper rolls still had their tissue covers on them. How often does one come across a virgin porta-john? Was this an act of God, Himself? I was movin' on up like George Jefferson. I had wind shelter, and I didn't need to go far to relieve myself. If I can use a toilet in place of a tent, someday I'll have to use a tent for a toilet and I'll have come full circle. Maybe after the holidays...

It was still tiny as a dog crate with my Big Green Monkey and myself crammed inside. In the middle of the night it occurred to me to use toilet paper as a makeshift weather stripping covering the airflow vents. I was Bob Villa for all of three minutes as I upgraded my living quarters. I didn't turn my Four Flush rated suite into a sauna, but I'm sure I helped dampen the effects of the cool air that was cycling freely previous to my efforts.

Sitting on the only chair in this shit hole, I had my notebook open on my lap. In my left hand I wielded a black ink pen, and in my right a button activated light that was part of my key chain. This is what all writers dream of: a cozy, professional atmosphere to work on their masterpiece.

If this little trip runs out of road as a result of limited resources, I suppose my luck could get me through a few nights, as it's shown. I hesitate relying on it for weeks, however. There's no telling where I'd be. If I burn off all my fuel heading away from here with nothing in reserve for an emergency retreat, I'd be in a real bind. What about water and food? There's no way I could lug enough weight to make it all the way across the deserts. I could use iodine tablet to create potable water, but I'd need to FIND water to do that with. Doing this right requires a spotter. They could take water out to me periodically, as needed. I don't even have so much as a BB gun to kill small game to eat, and irritate larger ones for my amusement. Snares are great if I were to remain in one spot long enough for them to produce results. The thing is, the longer I drag this out the more resources I'll exhaust. It's been my experience that slingshots are ineffective. In my youth I blasted a rabbit twice and the fluffy little bastard lived to hop another day.

This is far from the end of our epic. (Epics begin in the middle of things for those out there who slept through Literature class.) Far from it, my little cupcakes! I'm still in El Paso, and there's plenty left to do. It's difficult to tell what's coming next. "Always in motion is the future," as Obama's trusted campaign advisor would mention. There's a lot to be said for elderly, green Asian women.

My name is Daniel, meaning a "gift" from God. My middle, Michael, means "protector" of God. Thank you mom and dad. Name your next son, Howie or some shit. That way they'll feel less pressure and have lesser responsibilities.

Day 39: It is now November 12th. Throughout all the vicious, highly personal arguing Alice and I have been engaged in, never once did she say I couldn't do it. She knows from dealing with me that when I'm determined to do something I get it accomplished. The factor I need to consider is, at what cost? She believed in me albeit against the idea. There's a lot to be learned from that. Isn't that the type of thing you should go to the ends of the Earth to preserve?

I telephoned my parents and discussed options with them. It has been decided. I am scheduled to fly out of El Paso, Texas on November 25th. This situation, as it stands, will fail moving forward. A sponsor, or someone to act as a pace car, is necessary. I have the next 14 days to organize my notes, and take as many pictures of this beautiful horizon as I can.

This is all part of the premise. One must adapt to the ever-changing circumstances in order to be successful. I have come a very long way with little to none of the anticipated support. This trip was an incredible achievement, all things considered. I did myself proud, and I feel this was an admirable and honorable result.

The nights come earlier and it is getting much colder. I don't dare light a fire in my chosen crap dungeon. I'm not aware of the chemical contents in blue, porta-john solution. I'd hate to have this last chapter become part of a Darwin Awards publication after having blown myself up. The police report would be an interesting read: *White/Caucasian male, late twenties, found charred, dyed blue, and covered in piss and shit some forty yards from blast site.*

As far as accommodations go, this has been one of the best discoveries of the trip. It's roomier than some loft apartments in Manhattan. I once had a home with a nice toilet. Now I have a toilet for a home.

According to the friendly Mexican lady at the library, it's only eight miles to the airport. I haven't a choice but to trust her. After all, it says, "Information" on the sign hanging above her desk not, "Misguidance." The bus costs a dollar and a quarter. I need to transfer to another at the terminal, then make a proud one-mile walk into the Departures section of the airport.

There must have been a half-day at the nearby school. Droves of humans, some even shorter than myself, occupied the library making computer access impossible. I turned my attention to reading a few choice selections, found there was little of interest, and retreated back to Yucca Park. What was I doing here? Shouldn't I be wandering around with camera in hand shooting whatever sparks my interest?

If this whole book thing doesn't work out I may have to kill myself. That would mean I had the wrong idea about who I was my entire life. Anyone whose perception is that far off doesn't deserve to live. If not a writer, then what? I could see myself working for the DEA. I did drug interdiction in the Coast Guard and it's important for me to do something that matters. I'm sure I'd make a reliable government assassin if all other jobs were filled. I'd be employed by the secret government agencies we're not supposed to know about. What a rewarding career that would be! I'd get to travel a lot, see the world, and most, if not all, of my expenses would be covered. Remember, it's not a sin if your government tells you to do it. That brand of rationale worked wonders in Germany.

November 12<u>th</u>: Nightfall

There's a possibility I'll be spending less than 14 days here in El. It all hinges on whether or not I can get a standby seat on an earlier flight. The trouble is, I'm not sure how that works on flights other than that of the *non-stop* persuasion. I don't see how they could book both tickets upfront without regard to precedence for the would-be passengers at the second airport.

I'd like to get back as soon as possible, even though I know I belong out west. The more time I have to pin down a job or two, the more money I'll have by Christmas. Aside from the usual gift-giving duties, I'd like to fly Alice and the kids out to New York to see me. I don't know if she'll even accept the invitation, but I don't need reassurance to carry out these orders. I love her, and *our* kids. They only have one decent father figure in their lives and that's me. Poor bastards… It's time I reclaimed my role, one that I embraced immediately. It was as if it were meant to be. Now if only I could get along with their mother.

Alexander Stillwell wrote a book entitled, *Encyclopedia of Survival Techniques*. It's a fully illustrated rather generic, and vague guide at best. It probably took him a whole weekend of research to write his manual. The following information regarding the desert is extracted from the text in disjointed excerpts. This is all they had at the library on the topic. What do you want from me?

- "Daytime temperatures can reach 131 degrees in the shade, of which there is very little. At night the desert floor radiates the heat back, causing temperatures to drop near freezing. The temperature range ca be as great as 86 degrees F, and will vary considerably from one season to another…" *That my friends, is uninspired writing. Everyone is motivated. Some are just motivated to be lazy.*
- "Sandstorms are frequent and, apart from being extremely uncomfortable, they can also cause you to lose your bearings."
- "A characteristic of the desert is blinding glare."

- "Even in the coldest climate, 3.5 pints of water are lost every 24 hours. Add an extra 4.5 pints to that in a hot climate."
- "Mojave Rattlesnake: Deadly poisonous, found in Mojave Desert," *BIG SURPRISE,* "Nevada, Arizona, Texas, and New Mexico. Pale or sandy in color, diamond-shaped marks bordered by light colored scales and bands around the tail. Length: 2.5 ft avg, max 4ft"
- "Western Diamondback: Dangerously poisonous, AZ, Southeast California, NM, OK, TX. Light buff color with darker brown, diamond-shaped markings. Tail has thick black and white bands. Length: 5ft avg, max 6.5ft."

Basically, if you're going to get bitten, get bitten by the largest snake you can find. It seems to be better for your health. Just ask it to hold still a moment while you stretch out your measuring tape.

Once bitten the common treatment, aside from anti-venom which requires refrigeration, is to suck the poison out. There are kits sold in department stores in this part of the country made for this specific purpose. The advice they give is to make a small incision with the scalpel provided and *suck* the poison out. The POISON? What then? Something that can course through my veins and potentially kill me, only after causing nerve damage, making me lose control of my bowels, and inspiring my flesh to rot doesn't sound like the type of drink I'd want to order at the bar. With no Maytag Men in the desert, finding a nice, cold glass of anti-venom would be a challenge.

There's more data regarding ailments all starting with the word, *heat.* There are terms such as heat exhaustion, heat stroke, etc. Most involve the loss of one's mind, violent pain, vomiting, and death. I don't see the problem, yet.

Too many questions and a deficiency of answers… That's the feeling I'm left with having had the misfortune of cracking open that book. I'm not the type to give in to the easier, less impressive solution. Dying in a blaze of self-fulfilling glory, however, is an act left for the martyr. It can only be done once, so if it were a disappointing experience, it's too fucking late. My stubbornness and strong will has led me into difficult situations. I said *difficult* though, not impossible. I'd be breaking a personal record with a desert attempt. If this were a pole vault, there would be a need to raise the bar. I would be competing for the Gold in stupidity.

Did You Know: The origin of the word *fuck* is derived from an acronym? It stood for Fornication Under Consent of the King. Those with such license were mandated to place signs on their room doors with the letters, F.U.C.K. written on them. Did you hear that boys and girls? FUCK isn't a bad word. It's not even a word, at all. It's officially OK to say it freely and frequently. Run along now and practice what you've learned. Wow your parents, and impress your neighbors. Wait for the right moment and tell people your parents fear and respect all about it. I find a stuffy, high-tension dinner atmosphere to be perfect for this. Otherwise, try to visit your parents at work and tell their co-workers. Show them how smart you are! *This has been a public service announcement from Daniel Urbaetis.*

Even Later, same night, Nov 12th-13th: I took the last bus away from Yarbrough. The monkey rode for free. The driver informed me of the connection I needed to make at the terminal, and even phoned the other bus so they wouldn't depart until I was able to catch it. I arrived at the corner of Montana and Airways feeling energized from all of the positive social interaction. It doesn't take much to put me in a healthy mood. Common courtesy will do it almost every time. Somewhere ahead, under the blanket of night lies the airport. To my immediate right stands a Marriott Hotel with its red sign glowing confidently amidst the stars and streetlights.

Earlier in the day, my parents attempted to book a room for me using hotel points, but none were available. When given the option, it appears more people choose the Marriott over a porta-john. This explains the vacancies. I walked through the double glass doors, anyway. I've been lucky in places I've had no right being in for the full duration of the trip. Why should tonight be any different? Walking around a place like this with my Big Green

Monkey raises no eyebrows. Everyone has cargo in tow, or had it before ditching it in their rooms. The lobby's atmosphere was like walking into a silo that had been converted into a cathedral. Being short as it is, looking up at the chandelier in the center of the room was a glimpse into outer space. There were more artificial gold objects than one could count at a glance. Everything from trim work to hollow statues radiated with blinding, reflective light. Dark wood finish was the dominant wall color amidst the metallic dressings. When it was my turn, I explained to the pretty, Latin woman my situation. I found my eyes drawn to her gold nametag, among other things on her chest. It wasn't a particularly busy evening for the front desk. Most sane guests had already checked in for the night. She did a little research and confirmed there were no vacancies. "Is there anyone you'd like to see thrown out," I asked. There was a giggle, and then she pointed out the business center directly behind me in the oval room. She suggested I use the computer to "find a different hotel." Without *reservation*, I accepted counter offer.

There was only one other gentleman in the room when I made my way across the lobby. I couldn't help but notice how comfortable their brown leather couches and chairs looked as I passed them. Perhaps I'll sit and do a little writing afterward. I could always pantomime. If need be I could weasel out a little relaxation here, pretending to be waiting on a phone call or something bogus of that nature. The other person was quickly confirming his departure tickets and was gone before I could smell too much of his Aqua Velva.

Just as I logged into my site, I caught a glimpse of a head peeking around the doorframe in my peripherals. I looked toward the entrance and the head quickly vanished in a blur of color. I got up to inspect. There was only one person sitting on the couches without a jacket on. Not being a real patron, I felt it immoral to tie up facilities paying guests were interested in. I quickly logged back off and turned my efforts to finding the kid with the blurry face. I walked up to the jacketless man and asked if he was the one interested in using the computer. He confirmed he was, and I offered him the space to take care of whatever business he needed to tend to. It was my intention to get right back on, after he was finished, so I lingered between the couches and my Monkey that was still standing guard in the business center. As I was rifling through my monkey looking for my notebook, the man, now sitting at the computer desk struck up conversation. He asked me if I was still in the service and I gave him the two-minute summary about why I was there. He claimed he was ARMY, and therefore it was as if we knew one another. It's weird how some service members do that. Whether you're in or out, if you meet someone who's served, it's almost your obligation to become acquaintances. A common, scarring experience requires a large support group full of people who understand your pain, I suppose. I finished the conversation with details about my flight, and how I was going to roll the dice at the airport and hope to get home earlier than the 13 days. I asked him if there was something going on in town for the hotel to be booked. He said a lot of servicemen from the surrounding bases were on three days of leave before heading off into a different desert. His destination, along with many others, would be Iraq.

He offered to let me crash with him, sighting that he had a room with two beds. I didn't want to impose, especially on a brave, military member. I graciously declined, grabbed my Big Green Monkey, and headed toward the doors destined for the airport. I got about five feet into the fresh night air before it dawned on me that I was a retard. "What am I doing," I asked the stars in the sky. This guy just heard my situation, offered me a place to stay the night, and here I am wondering if I'll get a lucky break. What the hell am I doing outside? I doubled back to the tiny little office room and this time I was the guy peeking his head around the doorframe. "Two beds you say?"

It's amazing how thick headed I can be. Pride is another thing I need to tone down a bit. Everybody needs someone else's assistance. No on runs a business alone, no one makes a movie all by themselves. What I need to learn is that I make it far more difficult of a life, trying to do everything myself. I do so for good-natured reasons. I'm still a little shy, even at 29, but mainly I don't believe I deserve that which I cannot produce on my own. There is a lot of truth in that value, but sometimes like tonight, I had to see the forest from the trees. I was so locked into the problem that I didn't see a solution staring me right in the face. If I hadn't caught myself on time, I never would have slept comfortably nor would I have had the chance to use the shower in Room 356.

Day 40: Bob "Ski" Anuszewski, age 24, is an IT for the ARMY National Guard. As fate would have it, he is also my latest acquaintance on this journey. His family has a street named after them right off Route 146, no more than ten miles from where I lived. He revealed he was from Greenwich, NY, not far from where I was born and raised. We were practically neighbors in relative terms. I credit the five-year age difference and my stint, 3,000 miles away in the Coast Guard, for why we never met before. We had to come to El Paso, Texas of all places to meet for the first time. This is somewhat of a pattern for me. I didn't see my first Yankee game until I went to Safeco Field, and watched them beat the Mariners in Seattle.

In three days Bob will be flying into Iraq where he will be bravely serving our country for the next ten months. Being a Techie, with an impressive level of skills gained from both Siena College in Loudonville, New York, and from his extended military-specific training, Bob will not be in as much danger as say, Infantry would be. I am very relieved to have learned that, but there are still dangers and uncertainty. This isn't a trip to Dubai to play golf. Heading back as I am, I know I'd hear if something happened to a local hero. That is one newspaper I hope to never unfold.

I ask all who believe in this country, in the sacrifice good people make, and in humanity, to keep Bob and those like him in your thoughts as they serve their time in volatile lands. I feel like a better man for having met him. I can confidently walk away from this hotel feeling enriched and grateful for the experience. I almost robbed myself of an opportunity to meet someone whom I now admire. I feel proud, confident, and encouraged knowing that for every 1,000 morons from middle America who drag the service down, there is at least one guy like "Ski" on task. Intelligent, capable, and highly skilled people like him are the reason we, as a country, for the People have survived and prospered for so long.

It was refreshing and very unlikely I'd meet someone from my old stomping ground on a chance. Hopefully this will be the eve of my triumphant return. Bob knew about places such as

Pope's Pizza, in between Saratoga Springs and Ballston Spa, Siena College near my dad's house, and a dozen others. I needed this to calm my apprehension. A large part of me is lusting for desert sands and beyond. I've always wanted to be a Californian. I was introduced to the concept of being a filmmaker after seeing Reservoir Dogs at age 14, and since then it has been a dream of mine. It was only further reinforced when I spent time in both Southern and Northern California throughout my Coast Guard career. I've seen it and it was more than I could ever have hoped a place to be. California does not disappoint. It's not in its nature to do so. People may come with preconceived notions about who *they* are, and are let down when things don't pan out their way. That has nothing to do with the mountains or the valleys. It is a separate business, this artificial one. The real gem of the West is viewed from my perspective, as a man who wants nothing material. All I want to do is absorb as much of the scenery as I can before I die. A little recognition to validate my existence would be nice, but I only need enough money to lead a modest life, so long as I can work from a laptop as I sit, staring at the ocean. Perry Farrell said it best in Jane's Addiction, "I want to be more like the ocean... No talking and all action."

There's plenty of mountain scenery that has revealed itself with the rise of the Eastern sun. I will be determined to take some photographs after I beat the hell out of my body in the fitness center. A man must stay strong, not to mention handsome, does he not?

Perhaps my recent undertaking has taught me to look at things with the peripheral blinders off. I do this instinctively when I'm writing, but something is lost in translation to the world outside my own head. Always wrapped up in thought, I am. I know I'm a wiser person for having had these experiences. It's just the beginning of a whole new life I've opened myself up to, filled with fascinations and adventure yet discovered.

Daniel the Red Vested Bell Hop: I received an honorary nametag from Daniel, a foreign employee of this fine Marriott. There is no such animal as coincidence. What we need to concern ourselves with is what all the clues mean both in separate values and together. He was kind enough to take a few photos of me outside the establishment.

It seems I have a gift for traveling very inexpensively and relatively light given the duration. If I feel I made a mistake going back to New York, I could always pack up and leave in the middle of the night knowing I'd be able to survive with whatever supplies in my bag. The last thing I ever need to worry about is feeling trapped in a situation. No employer or relative has the power to hold anything over my head. God is my judge. I've taken the power back. I can remain there getting whatever I need accomplished, and allow them to think whatever helps them sleep at night. If they push me too hard, behave in a disrespectful fashion, try to manipulate me, or rob me of my time then I'll show them who's really in charge. Who the fuck do some people think they are? I'm looking for an excuse to let out my rage against ignorant, oppressive assholes. I'm no one's bitch, dear friends. Nothing can hurt me. Any attempt to would be a feeble one. If they push me to the point where I need to backpack it again, I'll be the one laughing. I thrive in this way of life. From hanging out with the lions I've gained their strength. I don't mind getting a little bloody and bruised so long as I decimate my opponent. I get off on the adrenaline from putting people in their place. I am not the type to take liberties with. For now I will remain docile. I need to gather income and afford myself time to write this book. The plan is to pay my uncle rent once I've acquired the job necessary to do so. I'll be living within 1.4 miles of major shit job locations, so I'll be able to walk to them and back. It can get well below freezing in the winter, so it will be the perfect environment to write in. I'll be free of the distractions most have living in places actually inhabitable by man.

"And one more special message to go
And then I'm done and I can go home
Love myself better than you
I know it's wrong, but what should I do…"

-

Nirvana, *On a Plane*

Flight 1084 to Georgia, then it's off to New York!

11:08 pm is the expected Eastern Standard ETA. I was fortunate to get this flight. It took a little luck, some chance, and an additional $150. If I hadn't jumped on it, I would have been loitering until after Thanksgiving. Just add it to my incredibly large tab, family... When and if I'm ever rich, I'll be broke again quickly. At least I'll have the burden of guilt off my shoulders leaving more room for my monkey.

The woman at the Delta check-in counter, Sandra B., had read Robert Perkin's book about his journey across America. It's one of her favorites, she claimed. She had abundant energy, the type I radiate when I discuss film and literature, so I took her for being sincere. When I told her of my recently completed adventure she was quite intrigued, asking me many detailed questions as if she were getting her family ready for a similar trip. I felt a certain amount of bashfulness and modesty slosh back and forth in my chest. If this is minutely similar to how it feels being famous, or being a guest on a talk show, I'm going to love it when it happens. A certain amount of discomfort is exciting. Recognition and acknowledgement are all I want. People needn't agree with my opinions. I'd rather they used their own heads. The fact that they are using them means they would have read my book, and therefore I caused them to have these thoughts. This is my goal in life. I want to share with the world the nonstop flood of ideas always saturating my mind. I don't want to keep it all to myself, especially if I can make positive, progressive change come about in someone else's existence. I just need a publisher to allow me to share with the world what is rightfully theirs. The ideas aren't uniquely mine. It's my belief that a muse, like a radio signal, broadcasts the message to everyone. I just happened to be tuned on certain stations others are not, and they, tuned to ones I am not. That is why we converge to share what we've been receiving so we all may digest it, and absorb it for what it's worth. It's the last thing we still do as a community in this increasingly impersonal, technological society.

The paparazzi would love me. I understand a person's need for privacy. I respect it more than one could ever imagine. I am a very private person. For me, however, I'm too friendly to let a picture or a dozen get to me. So long as they weren't shouting insults to my family or myself they'd have me as their ally. If they wanted pictures to sell so they could make a living, I would cooperate. I'm sure not all of these people are piranhas. Some must have wives and families to feed. Think about it for a moment. You are an amateur photographer with dreams of being the next Ansel Adams, but for now you have bills to pay. The only way to do that is to be aggressive. I'm sure some ethics and morals are bent in this profession, like all others. People who wouldn't normally go to the lengths they are going do so out of the same desperation a guy at a mortgage company who fudged one document has. Whatever, I'm poor and not famous, but I still get it. We're all people. We all tick for mostly the same reasons. Compassion is a virtue I have an abundance of in place of patience and forgiveness.

Too bad MC Escher wasn't available to illustrate this book. I bet he'd have fun with it. Son-of-a-bitch won't answer his phone, so I'm forced to deprive my readers of such a luxury.

Sandra B. tried her heart out to find me a flight at no additional cost, as her fingers were a blur over her keyboard from moving so swiftly. Me, I hunt and peck with the best of them and look at the profession I've chosen! I'm much more at home with a pen. I'm probably the last, fairly young author, who still appreciates the old school way of things. I *will* be the last as new generations are born into a more technologically advanced atmosphere. If flight 1084 hadn't been delayed en route, I would never have made it onboard before departure. It was originally scheduled for 1:03 pm, but as luck and God would have it, its new arrival time was anticipated for 2:10 pm. Due to the heavy, make-a-buck restrictions placed on online ticket purchases, I had no choice but to relay this information to my mother via Delta desk phone. That should bring my total bill to about $250,000. If I do not become famous, I'll have the debt paid in full in no more than 60 years, tops. I should really push for a camping line or shoe endorsement contract, if nothing else. If the coverage were there in the beginning, the sponsors and media would have created the fame to market afterward, themselves. I tried to tell them…

I felt like an asshole checking in my Big Green Monkey. There's no air in those compartments! Is he going to be OK? We looked at one another, no words spoken. We've become so close we know what the other is thinking. He gave me that look like, "Go get on that plane, soldier. I'm proud of ya!" I nodded that I understood and released him as the lady who was struggling to put the Monkey on the conveyer belt, finally broke him free of my grip and stumbled backward slightly. I swear I saw a single teardrop fall fro my Big Green Monkey like the famous old commercial with the Native American portrayed by a white actor in a headdress.

Many thoughts rushed though my head as I made my way up the escalator and found the appropriate boarding gate. There was a maze of confusion, as per usual, with many people more determined than I, scurrying about to make their flights. There's always a high concentration of beautiful women in these settings. It's difficult not to stare, if only for a momentary distraction. It didn't seem so dire that I made it home once I was sitting at my gate awaiting my section to be called. I was filled with a feeling of indifference. What challenges could normal life throw at me after all I've experienced? Was I destined for boredom? I know I was doing the smart thing, but I'm more of the balls-in-open-air type of guy. I'm willing to risk every last drop of mine, and other's blood to complete a mission. My zone, number 9, was announced.

"Will I ever get to where I'm going
If I do will I know when I am there
If the wind blew me in the right direction
Could I even care?"

Incubus

Three hours of midair travel and I'll be in a different time zone. I'll only be in Georgia, but I'll be on the appropriate coast for my final destination. I don't like that word, *final* in this context. It's too absolute. Besides, it doesn't sound nearly as handsome and poetic as when Regis Philben says it in his catch phrase, "Final Answ!?"

I never knew that man was a fellow Italian. There aren't enough vowels in his last name to make it obvious. I smell deception. I'm on to you, Regis.

This is *not* my "final" destination…

"Because what I want and what I need is and will always be free…"

-

Incubus, *When It Comes*

I'm in seat 17C by fate, luck, and God's guiding hand. There is no logical reason why I should have been able to catch this plane. Imagine if you will, all of the circumstances that had to line up today to make this seat mine. I was intended to leave 13 long days from now, there were no seats left on the connector flight awaiting me in Georgia, save one. This plane, having arrived late, set the stage for all other details to come to fruition. It makes me wonder whether this aircraft is targeted for its demise. Will I succumb to a Big Bopper ending?

If it be my fate, then so be it. God's plan is not for me to judge, question, or be afraid of. That last bit is important. If I'm struck down I will arise with more strength than any living man could ever hope to fathom. Phoenix—reborn. The dark angel, with sins like dander trapped in his feathers, making him almost human as he protects the virtuous in the night skies… That will be my next adventure. Doing God's work doesn't mean you have to be a pussy. That's just what they sell at Christian money thieving assemblies. I believe the feeling in my heart over any utterance of Man.

As the break is released on the plane, giving license to a slight jolt and rocking motion, I strongly sense a divine presence. Why you ask? I'm conjuring it. I'm forcing Him to be here and pay close attention to the proceedings. If he wants me to continue working for Him, there are certain things I require from Him. Do you see what I meant when I said I was too much trouble for the demons to bother with? I'm riding the fucking line between heaven and hell. On one side I'm giving high-fives and pulling people up with me. On the other side I'm driving my fist in the faces of those looking to corrupt the good people just across that thin line. I choose how long I ride, and I choose the terms. I'd never work for the other side, and He knows that. Just how involved I get in His work, however, depends on how He chooses to sweeten the pot. I am in a position to negotiate at the highest level. That whole government assassin thing is sounding better and better as we taxi the airport.

Have a seat, Lord. What have you got to offer? At the very least, what's my next assignment? Allow me to remain idle, and I'll create my own missions.

I've been absorbing surrounding conversations. The man sitting directly behind me works to protect military vehicles from I.E.D.s. I am among good, patriotic people. There are members of various armed service divisions scattered about the aircraft wearing their best stars and straps. This is a message, but it's just saying, "Hello, brother. Welcome aboard." There is a sense of warmth in this tiny space. If this were my time, I could think of worse company to follow me to the afterlife. They would likely continue on to heaven, whereas I'd be on immediate assignment.

I find it peculiar that my strengths are perceived as weaknesses to most of the flock. I am not broken, nor do I need fixing. I'm born offensive. I'll die being offensive. I make no apologies if you don't get the punch line. I have all of the validation I need from within. Outward approval is a drug for the desperate.

This is the path that works for me without me having to even question it. It's not for everyone, but don't be discouraged. There are many ways to arrive to the same, desired results. Just because someone finds a way, they think it's the only way. Hence civilization was born. If your path feels right keep on it. If it doesn't, change it before you're snuffed out or it becomes dull. Remember, all roads do not lead to Eden.

Wisdom comes from understanding that you will never know a goddamn thing for certain. It encapsulates both the desirable and undesirable outcomes. Fighting against that is an exercise for the immature and we're all guilty to some extent. Many replace wisdom with knowledge, thinking if they devote themselves completely to one, they can ignore the other all together. Good luck with that…

I used to place a lot of importance on the wrong things. What's worse is I was dependent on one system, one path, and one encompassing idea about how life should be lived to come through for me.

I see things with a clarity I would never have obtained, never have earned, if not for this trip. I will take from life what it does not give freely. I have become strong enough to do so. This is not some faggy, *roll the dice and hope for the best* attempt at life. Gamblers expect loss. I am not a gambler. I don't expect, nor do I accept any type of loss unless I see a way to play an angle off it for even greater gains.

All of you owe it to yourself to exit the casino and take a chance on *you*, rather than the rigged game. You might surprise yourself… Perhaps it is I who will be reading your book in the future.

Georgia to Albany, NY: After no real time at all I'm, again, seated in an airplane. This time it's called 14D and it's flush against the emergency exit! We were debriefed. During the lecture I took some attitude from the bitchy flight attendant. Negative attitudes and rudeness hunger a crushing fist. Someone should be delivering corrective adjustments to incorrect behavior. I would never dare to be that condescending to another human being. If I did, I'd anticipate my earned beating. Of course, I'm sort of an absolute psychopath when it comes to being proper. I support capital punishment for those in opposition to, or ignorant of it.

This woman, with her bow tied so tight it was cutting off circulation of proper judgment to her brain, asked me to confirm that I could do everything stated on the list in case of an emergency. She was holding it and waving it about. I can't read small print from three and a half feet away. While everyone else, obviously eagle-eyed speed-readers, shouted out their responses, I was trying to make out what was written. She became statuesque. Great, maybe now I can read the fucking pamphlet. Immediately she began shouting, "OK? OK?" Just for that, if something does happen, I'm popping off this door and riding it like a magic carpet. I'll be Little Nemo and his bed, coasting in a spiral flight pattern before gently touching down on the ground.

"If you want me to give you an honest answer, I'd have to actually read what it says, ma'am."

She rolled her eyes and I felt everyone else's glare. "OK, fine. Yes. Happy? If there's any mention of anal sex, bench pressing a bulldozer, or squad thrusts in there, I *will* retract my involvement during the emergency leaving all of you to fend for yourselves." I got two laughs and double the amount of dirty looks. This should be a fun flight. Can't wait!

Through her haste, she made her problems and her stress mine. What are women for? I was put in a position to have to lie because this is society again. It's right here on the plane. Nothing has value and everything is for show. Whatever, as Tim Armstrong sings, "And I know I'm indestructible!" Honesty is the least of society's vaules. Real truth and honesty are actually the greatest threats to it, so it's better to just keep those things under its fingernail. I once said to a friend, "The best liar always tells the truth."

Day MOTHERFUCKING 41:

"The future's uncertain and the end is always near."
                              -The Doors, *Roadhouse Blues*

"I need a brand new friend who doesn't bother me
I need a brand new friend who doesn't trouble me
I need somebody who doesn't need me…"

                              -The Doors, *Hyacinth house*

Well, after feeling like my heart was being ripped out of my ribcage in a slightly different manner everyday for the last year I'm still not hopping off this pony ride. Even if the pony had one eye and three legs in its best days. Please enjoy my super happy friendship rainbow poem:

Her hand clenches my heart causing a weak and muffled beat. The color leaves my face as each breath is more shallow than the last. Pain, as sharp as roasted needle tips, puncture my vital organs in the otherwise numbing blanket of asphyxiation. My temples

pound like dual base drums. I can no longer think clearly…
Delirium. I'm drifting into a darkness much colder than
anticipated. There is no comforting detachment. I am locked
within the moment, forced to feel everything with no shield, no
protection. I drown in the hollow blackness of her doomed heart
as her icy claws dig into my flesh and pull me, lifeless, into the
abyss of consequence.

I had to get the last few months off my chest. Poetry is a
far better solution than murder-suicide. Besides, when it comes to
those I love or loved, I do what I can to protect them. Never would
I hurt them. It doesn't matter if an ex-love or a family member
wronged me in the worse way. In their time of need, I'd be the
vigilante fucking shit up and placing the severed heads of their
oppressors on sticks. That's just how I operate. I keep the higher
ground. That's why I have earned the right to fart under the covers
and pull the blanket over my head for a whiff of sweet divinity.

I miss my dog. I'm living in a frozen tundra, 1,500 miles
from the woman I love, the kids my heart has adopted, and the
aforementioned fleabag. What a fool this mortal be.

I have been through many a battle to complete two very
important tests. One was of the heart, the other of the soul. I aced
both. If I hadn't aced them I would have received no score at all
for lack of participation. That's where I see most people headed
who ignore what's most important.

I learned there's virtue in being a gutter punk, if you had
my set of values going in, I mean. I learned that God takes all
kinds and is just as disgusted with the Jesus-Rainbow society as I
am. He needs soldiers. The war is coming. Stop selling peace and
togetherness. We get it. It's time we armed ourselves to the
fucking teeth. Fuck the rules of Man. They won't save you when
all of Man is thrown to the fire to see which of us burn. They want
to be Satan's bitch, that's their business. I'll take their worthless
heads off when the time comes—should they cross my path. I may
even resort to cannibalism when the doomed have cut down the
last tree, poisoned the water, and eradicated all other animals from
the planet. Better drink plenty, now. You'll be thirsty. Greatest
ally or worse enemy, there is no in between with me.

Imagine a life free of fear and doubt. Hold onto your regrets and guilt. That's what differentiates us from the evil ones. We maintain a sense of right and wrong. The devil sells freedom all the while enslaving those foolish enough to be tempted. Real freedom is in the third realm the books don't talk about. We are the mercenaries, God's soldiers for hire. We do what the devout are too weak to do on their own. We get our hands dirty. God wouldn't dare damn us for saving his flock in their time of need. The devil wouldn't dare allow us to infect his safe haven. Where does that leave us? Eternal reincarnation, my friends. We're the recycled rejects of both realms and we wouldn't have it any other way. Heaven would become too dull, and Hell would be too much work, albeit engaging. No, we live among the demons and saints on planet Earth. This place is what makes sense to us. When looking from a mountaintop at a red and purple sky, we have our heaven. When we raise families and feel loved, our warrior hearts are complete. We are a simple breed, requiring little to satisfy us. The funny thing is, what we value is what's most important. God may have started off as one of us, evolved, and retired. What is for certain is he bred us for battle. It's sad to think some of us have forgotten that. The breed within the breed... We are like the Scottish in a way. Point us toward conflict and we'll get the job done.

Not all will understand what I say. I'm sure half or more will think I should be committed. There will be a percentage who will feel their hearts for the first time, however. They might be in bed with this book on bent knees reading into the night when something happens inside them—a whisper. Will it be enough to awaken them? Will they take the initiative and make the next step on their own? Perhaps... Like I said, I am a warrior. I'm not cut out for this inspirational bullshit. I, like R. P. McMurphy in *One Flew Over the Cukoo's Nest*, am here because I fight and fuck too much. And to those two values I am an artist.

I stepped up to the challenge and accepted my calling. Not everyone is meant for this, so if you are tuned to a different frequency, your role is just as valid and important. I can only speak of that which I know and understand. I'm just part of a certain batch of sea monkeys in God's collection.

You know what they say, "Those who can *do*. Those who can't host Inside the Actor's Studio." I'm onto you, Mr. James Lipton. Rip Torn called. He wants his DNA back.

Don't be afraid of your own power. Do not be afraid to succeed and conquer. Your only limitations are those that are self-imposed. Think and Execute. Even better, think less and execute more frequently. What are you waiting for? Remember what I said. You might surprise yourself.

It should be mentioned that a plan should always be devised first. Be smart, but give license to valid influences and circumstances that inspire alteration. Ride the wave, but do so intelligently. Always calculating is the successful mind, but do not be consumed by the unimportant details that drown the inner voice. Room must be reserved for abstract thought and that which cannot be ascertained on the conscious level. This is vital to the evolution of an event's meaning and substance within the mind. It is the only way one can achieve a personal connection to an experience and maybe, just maybe feel less alone in this vast universe of consequence. Optimism, whether we want to acknowledge it or not, is necessary for our survival. My far more intelligent, younger brother could write a series of books, himself, on the importance of this aspect.

The Divided Highway: a final note

We have come to the book's end, but the road goes on…
The path continues to wind. This isn't the end nor the beginning
for the Divided Highway has neither. It simply *is* and that's its
mystique. That is what intrigues us and excites our hearts.

We catch up with it in the middle of things, like a Greek
Epic, and take it for as long as we can. We expect certain things;
like a better understanding, gained wisdom, and experiences. The
Divided Highway does not disappoint. It may, however, deliver on
these desires in a way we never expected or planned for. This is
the virtue it keeps all to itself. It has the will to do its duty
whichever way it sees fit. We cannot control the Divided
Highway's nature, for it is older and wiser. Only *it* knows how to
get through to us. We walk out there as children and come back,
maybe not as men, but with a deeper understanding of what should
be valued and what is most important.

May your journey in life involve a considerable level of
risk and uncertainty. What some perceive as unfavorable is truly a
blessing in disguise. Remember I will be there with you in spirit
just as those I quoted were there for me. I want you to succeed and
I will take personal interest in those brave enough to take on this
mission. I cannot live for you, however. You have an obligation
to yourself to accomplish that.

Thank you Dad for your priceless love and guidance.
Thank you Gram for always being a tremendous source of love and
virtue. Thank you Pa for all your inherited dry humor, your big
heart and great wisdom. Thank you Aunt Gina, for loving me as if
I was your own son. You and Gram left us too soon, but I have no
doubt we'll catch up to you on a different road someday. They all
taught me to give love out. It's just what you do. And when you
do, it comes back to you exponentially.

God bless you all. It took me a long time to say those
words aloud, but I always felt them in my heart. God is what you
make of it—so is heaven. Be open to the warmth of this world and
you will always smile a sincere, happy smile.

With Much Love and
Respect,

~Daniel

www.ingramcontent.com/pod-product-compliance
Lightning Source LLC
Chambersburg PA
CBHW070044260626
47159CB00005B/2118